PRAISE FOR
12 DAYS AT BLEAKLY

A Victorian treasure filled with atmospheric mystery, humor, romance, unexpected twists, and quirky characters that would make Charles Dickens proud. Michelle Griep has penned a winner!

—Julie Klassen, bestselling, award-winning author

Hands down, the most fun I've had reading a book in a long time! With a plot reminiscent of a mystery dinner theater, the author gathers a cast of characters you will not soon forget into an English manor where murder, mayhem, and mystery ensue. Add in a speck of romance and a sprinkle of humor, and you have a masterpiece of literary entertainment.

—MaryLu Tyndall, award-winning author of the Legacy of the King's Pirates series

Fans of Victorian Era romance will swoon over *12 Days at Bleakly Manor: Book 1 in Once Upon a Dickens Christmas* by Michelle Griep. Her characters are mesmerizing, her writing flawless—a winning combination!

—Elizabeth Ludwig, author of *A Tempting Taste of Mystery*

Book 1 in the Once Upon a Dickens Christmas series

12 DAYS AT BLEAKLY MANOR

MICHELLE GRIEP

SHILOH RUN PRESS
An Imprint of Barbour Publishing, Inc.

Print ISBN 978-1-68322-258-3

eBook Editions:
Adobe Digital Edition (.epub) 978-1-68322-515-7
Kindle and MobiPocket Edition (.prc) 978-1-68322-516-4

Cover Design: Kirk DouPonce, DogEared Design

Published by Shiloh Run Press, an imprint of Barbour Publishing, Inc., P.O. Box 719, Uhrichsville, Ohio 44683, www.shilohrunpress.com

Our mission is to publish and distribute inspirational products offering exceptional value and biblical encouragement to the masses.

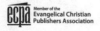

Member of the
Evangelical Christian
Publishers Association

Printed in Canada.

On a stormy night
two thousand years ago,
a babe was born
and in a land far from that rugged stable
a coin was forged ~
both the bearers of a second chance.

The God-man returned to heaven,
but the coin yet roams the earth,
passing from hand to hand,
hope to hope. . .

The First Day
DECEMBER 24, 1850

Chapter One

London, 1850

Christmas or not, there was nothing merry about the twisted alleys of Holywell. Clara Chapman forced one foot in front of the other, sidestepping pools of. . .well, a lady ought not think on such things, not on the morn of Christmas Eve—or any other morn, for that matter.

Damp air seeped through her woolen cape, and she tugged her collar tighter. Fog wrapped around her shoulders, cold as an embrace from the grim reaper. Though morning had broken several hours ago, daylight tarried, seeming reluctant to make an appearance in this part of London—and likely wishing to avoid it altogether. Ancient buildings with rheumy windows leaned toward one another for support, blocking a good portion of the sky.

She quickened her pace. If she didn't deliver Effie's gift soon, the poor woman would be off to her twelve-hour shift at the hatbox factory.

Rounding a corner, Clara rapped on the very next door, then fought the urge to wipe her glove. The filthy boards, hung together more by memory than nails, rattled like bones. Her lips pursed into a wry twist. A clean snow might hide the sin of soot and grime in this neighborhood, but no. Even should a fresh coating of white bless all, the stain of so much humanity would not be erased. Not here. For the thousandth time, she breathed out the only prayer she had left.

Why, God? Why?

The door swung open. Effie Gedge's smile beamed so bright and familiar, Clara's throat tightened. How she missed this woman, her friend, her confidant—her former maid.

"Miss Chapman? What a surprise!" Effie glanced over her shoulder, her smile faltering as she looked back at Clara. "I'd ask you in but. . ."

Clara shoved away the awkward moment by handing over a basket. "I've brought you something for your Christmas dinner tomorrow. It isn't much, but…" It was Clara's turn to falter. "Anyway, I cannot stay, for Aunt's developed a cough."

Effie's smile returned, more brilliant than ever. "That's kind of you, miss. Thank you. Truly."

The woman's gratitude, so pure and genuine, rubbed Clara's conscience raw. Would that she might learn to be as thankful for small things. And small it was. Her gaze slipped to the cloth-covered loaf of bread, an orange, and used tea leaves wrapped in a scrap of paper. Pressing her lips together, she faced Effie. "I wish it were more. I wish *I* could do more. If only we could go back to our old lives."

"Begging your pardon, miss." Effie rested her hand on Clara's arm, her fingers calloused from work no lady's maid should ever have to perform. "But you are not to blame. I shall always hold to that. There is no ill will between us."

Clara hid a grimace. Of course she knew in her head she wasn't to blame, but her heart? That fickle organ had since reverted to her old way of thinking, pulsing out *"you are unloved, you are unwanted"* with every subsequent beat.

"Miss?"

Clara forced a smile of her own and patted the woman's hand. "You are the kind one, Effie. You've lost everything because of my family, and yet you smile."

"The Lord gives, and the Lord takes away. I suppose you know that as well as I, hmm?" Her fingers squeezed before she released her hold. "I wish you merry, Miss Chapman, this Christmas and always."

"Thank you, Effie. And a very merry Christmas be yours, as well." She spun, eyes burning, and pushed her way back down the narrow alley before Effie saw her tears. This wasn't fair. None of it.

Her hired hansom waited where she'd left it. The cab was an expense she'd rather not think on, but altogether necessary, for she lived on the other side of town. She borrowed the driver's strong grip to ascend onto the step, then when inside, settled her skirts on the seat while he shut the door.

Only once did she glance out the window as the vehicle jostled along London's rutted roads—and immediately repented for having done so. Two lovers walked hand in hand, the man bending close and whispering into the woman's ear. A blush then, followed by a smile.

Clara yanked shut the window curtain, the loneliness in her heart rabid and biting.

That could have been her. That *should* have been her.

Why, God? Why?

She leaned her head back against the carriage. Was love to be forever denied her? First her father's rejection, then her fiancé's. She swallowed back a sob, wearier than twenty-five years ought to feel.

Eventually the cab jerked to a halt, and she descended to the street. She dug into her reticule and pulled out one of her last coins to pay the driver. At this rate, she wouldn't have to hire a cab to visit Effie next Christmas. She might very well be her neighbor.

"Merry Christmas, miss." The driver tipped his hat.

"To you, as well," she answered, then scurried toward Aunt's town house. A lacquered carriage, with a fine pair of matched horses at the front, stood near the curb. Curious. Perhaps the owner had taken a wrong turn, for Highgate, while shabbily respectable, was no Grosvenor Square.

Clara dashed up the few stairs and entered her home of the last nine months, taken in by the charitable heart of her Aunt Deborha Mitchell. The dear woman was increasingly infirm and housebound, but in her younger days she'd hobnobbed with people from many spheres.

Noontide chimes rang from the sitting-room clock, accompanied by a bark of a cough. Clara untied her hat and slipped from her cloak, hanging both on a hall tree, all the while wondering how best to urge Aunt back to her bed. The woman was as stubborn as. . . She bit her lower lip. Truth be told, tenacity ran just as strongly in her own veins.

Smoothing her skirts, she pulled her lips into a passable smile and crossed the sitting room's threshold. "I am home, Aunt, and I really must insist you retire—oh! Forgive me."

She stopped at the edge of the rug. A man stood near the mantel, dressed in deep blue livery. Her gaze flickered to her aunt. "I am sorry. I did not know you had company."

"Come in, child." Aunt waved her forward, the fabric of her sleeve dangling too loosely from the woman's arm. "This involves you."

The man advanced, offering a creamy envelope with gilt writing embellishing the front. "I am to deliver this to Miss Clara Chapman. That is you, is it not?"

She frowned. "It is."

He handed her the missive with a bow, then straightened. "I shall await you at the door, miss."

Her jaw dropped as he bypassed her, smelling of lavender of all things. She turned to Aunt. "I don't understand."

"I should think not." Aunt nodded toward the envelope. "Open it."

Clara's name alone graced the front. The penmanship was fine. Perfect, actually. And completely foreign. Turning it over, she broke the seal and withdrew an embossed sheet of paper, reading aloud the words for Aunt to hear.

> *The Twelve Days of Christmas**
> *As never's been reveled*
> *Your presence, Miss Chapman,*
> *Is respectfully herald.*
> *Bleakly Manor's the place*
> *And after twelve nights*
> *Five hundred pounds*
> *Will be yours by rights.*

She lowered the invitation and studied her aunt. Grey hair pulled back tightly into a chignon eased some of the wrinkles at the sides of her eyes, yet a peculiar light shone in the woman's faded gaze. Aunt Deborha always hid wisdom, but this time, Clara suspected she secreted something more.

"Who sent this?" Clara closed the distance between them and knelt in front of the old woman. "And why?"

Aunt shrugged, her thin shoulders coaxing a rumble in her chest. A good throat clearing staved off a coughing spell—for now. "One

---

* Brief explanations of historical traditions mentioned throughout this story can be found on pages 183–184.

does not question an opportunity, my dear. One simply mounts it and rides."

"You can't be serious." She dissected the tiny lift of Aunt's brows and the set of her mouth, both unwavering. Incredible. Clara sucked in a breath. "You think I should go? To Bleakly Manor, wherever that is?"

"I think"—Aunt angled her chin—"you simply must."

CHAPTER TWO

Running an absent finger over the burnt scabs on his forearm, Benjamin Lane sagged against the cell's stone wall, welcoming the sharp sting of pain. It wouldn't last long. The crust would fall away, leaving a series of black numbers etched into his skin. A permanent mark, forever labeling him a convict to be feared, and driving a final stake through the heart of his efforts to be something in this world. Turning aside, he spit out the sour taste in his mouth, then his lips curled into a snarl. He was something, all right.

An outcast.

Anger rose in him like a mad dog, biting and completely impotent, for he had no idea who'd put him in this rat hole. The only thing he did know, he wished he didn't. Not now. Not ever. Growling roared in his ears. Was that him? *Oh, God.* Not again.

Betrayal from an enemy he could understand, but from the woman he loved? What man could fathom that? For nine months he'd turned that question over and over, examining every angle, each nuance, and still he could not reckon Clara's duplicity.

Why, God? Why?

A finger at a time, Ben opened his hand and stared fiercely at a small chunk of stone, barely discernable in the darkness. Worn smooth now by nearly a year of caressing. He flipped it over, just like his unanswered questions, the sleekness of the rock against his palm reminding him he was human, not beast. Outside his cell, a shriek crawled beneath the crack in his door, reaching for him, taunting him to believe otherwise. To join the howl and become one with the pack of hopeless men.

He flipped the rock again. The movement tethered him to sanity. Cocking his head, he listened with his whole body. Something more than screams crept in. The scrape of boot leather. Growing louder. Metal on metal, key battling key. The low murmur of a coarse jest shared between two guards.

Sweat popped out on Ben's forehead. He pressed his back into the wall, an impossible wish to disappear digging into his gut. The footsteps stopped. Only a slab of scarred wood separated him from his tormentors. Some Christmas this would be.

The key jiggled in the lock, and his stomach twisted. It was safer to remain here. In the dark. At least in this womb of crumbling brick and blackness he still heard the cries of other prisoners, as regular as a mother's heartbeat. He yet felt the dampness of rot on his skin, tasted the rancid gruel served once a day. Still breathed. Still lived.

He flipped the rock again.

The door swung open. A lantern's glow silhouetted two ghouls.

One stepped forward, a club in his grasp. "Out with ye, Lane. Warden's got a little Christmas gift with yer name on it."

Ben wrapped his fingers tight around the stone. Should he make a run for it? Spring an attack and wrestle for the club? Go limp? He'd sigh, if he had any breath to spare, but even that seemed a precious commodity nowadays.

No, better to face this head-on and not relinquish the last morsel of his dignity. He shuffled forward, the chains on his feet rasping. Shackles bit a fresh wound into his ankles with each step.

Leaving behind the only haven he'd known the past nine months, he stumbled into the corridor, guards at his back, prodding, poking. He lurched along, passing other doors, other convicts, inhaling the stench and guilt of Millbank Prison. How many wretches as innocent as he perished behind those doors?

One foot. Then the other. Drag, step. Drag, step. Until the stairway. The weight of his chains pulled him back as he ascended. By the time he reached the top, blood trickled hot over his feet.

"Move it!"

The guard's club hit between his shoulder blades, knocking him forward and jarring loose his precious stone. It clacked onto the floor, as loud to him as the hammer pounding in Christ's nails, then bounced down the stairs, taking his soul along with it.

No!

He wheeled about, diving for his only remainder of hope.

But a boot caught him in the gut. A club cracked against his skull. Half-lugged, half-dead, he landed in the warden's office like an alley cat thrown against a curb. The warden's sigh barely registered.

"Don't know why I expected anything different. Thank you, gentlemen. You may wait outside. Up you go, Lane." Warden Hacksby extended a hand.

Ignoring the offer, Ben sucked in a breath and forced his body up, staggering until the room stopped spinning.

"If nothing else, you are consistent." Hacksby chuckled and seated himself behind a desk as angular as the man himself. "Do you know what day it is?"

Ben worked out the soreness in his jaw before words could escape. "Sorry. I'll have to check my calendar and get back to you. Or. . .wait a minute. Ahh, yes. Am I to sail for Australia today?" He narrowed his eyes. "But we both know I'll never reach the shore."

"Ever the cynic, eh? Really, Lane. After all the hospitality I've shown you." Hacksby tut-tutted, the curl of his lip exposing yellowed teeth. "But no. There's been a change of plans. You've received another offer, should you choose to take it."

Bitterness slipped from Ben's throat in a rusty laugh. "What, the gallows? A firing squad? Or has Queen Victoria invited me for Christmas tea?"

"Aha! So you do know what day it is. Always the sly one, are you not?" Hacksby rose from his seat and leaned across the desk, a creamy envelope with Ben's name in golden script on the front. "For you. Your freedom, possibly—providing you play by the rules. If not, you're to be shot on sight for any escape attempt."

Ben eyed the paper. What trick was this? He was supposed to be transported to a labor camp halfway across the world, not handed an engraved invitation. He stiffened. This was a trap. He knew it to the deepest marrow in his bones.

Nevertheless, he reached out, and for the smallest of moments, the warden held one edge, he the other. Liberty hanging in the balance.

Maybe.

CHAPTER THREE

Despite her cold fingers, Clara rubbed away the frost on the coach's window, then peered out into the December night. She ought be sore by now, riding such a distance over country roads, but truly, this carriage was magnificent—and so was the mansion that popped into view as they rounded a bend. She leaned closer, then reared back as her breath fogged the glass. With a furious swipe of her glove, she stared out the cleared circle, slack jawed.

This was Bleakly Manor?

A grand structure, torches ablaze, lit the night like the star of Bethlehem. The building stood proud at three stories tall, with candles winking behind row upon row of mullioned windows. Clearly whoever owned Bleakly didn't care a fig about window taxes. Clara held her breath and edged closer, careful not to muddle her view with rime. Garland swagged from the roofline the entire length of the building. How on earth had they managed that? Red bows with dangling ribbons hung from each wall sconce, and as the carriage drew nearer, a gust of wind lent them life, and they waved a greeting.

She sat back against the cushion, stunned. There was nothing bleak about this manor. Who had invited her—a lowly lady's companion—to such an estate? Who would even want to keep company with her? And more importantly, why?

The coach stopped, and the door opened. She gave up trying to solve such a puzzle as the footman helped her to the drive.

"I'll see to your bags, miss." A lad, no more than fourteen yet dressed in as fine a livery as the older man, tipped his head in deference.

The respectful gesture stung. She hadn't been so favored since that awful day, that nightmare day nine months previous, when she'd stood in front of an altar in a gown of white.

"Ready, miss?"

The footman's voice pulled her from the horrid memory. She lifted her skirts to follow him without tripping. "Yes."

She was ready, truly, to meet whoever had invited her. Perhaps if she explained the frail state of her aunt, she wouldn't be required to stay the full Twelve Days of Christmas.

After ascending granite stairs, she and the footman passed through an arched doorway and entered a foyer the size of Aunt's dining and sitting rooms combined. A crystal chandelier dripped golden light over everything, from a cushioned bench against one wall to a medieval trestle table gracing the other. Fresh flowers filled a cut-glass vase atop the table. Marble tile gleamed beneath her feet, the echo of her steps reaching up to a mounted lion head on the wall in front of her, just above a closed set of doors. She couldn't help but stare up into the cold, lifeless eyes, wondering how many people before her had done the same.

"I should be happy to take your cloak and bonnet, miss." The footman held out his arm.

Her fingers shook as she unbuttoned her coat and untied her hat, though she was hard-pressed to decide if the jittery feeling was from cold air or nerves. Handing over her garments, she waited for further instruction from the tall fellow.

But without a word, he pivoted and disappeared down a darkened hallway to her left.

She stood, unsure, and clenched her hands for fortification, sickeningly aware of a gaze burning holes through her soul. Yet the only other pair of eyes in the foyer besides hers was the lion's.

She sucked in a breath. Nerves. That's what. Had to be.

To her right, another set of doors hid secrets, merry ones by the sound of it. Yellow light and conversation leached out through a crack between threshold and mahogany. Licking her lips, she squared her shoulders, resolved to meet the master of the house, then pushed open the door.

Across the Turkish carpet, perched upon a chair and balancing a small box on her lap, a white-haired lady held up a quizzing glass to one eye and peered at Clara. "Oh, lovely! Such a beautiful creature. Don't you think, Mr. Minnow?"

"Why yes!" A lean man, more bones than flesh, jumped up from a settee and dashed toward Clara so quickly she retreated a step.

He bowed, deep enough that his joints cracked, and held the pose longer than necessary. The scent of ginger wafted about him. When he straightened, he smiled at her with lips that were far too elastic. "Mr. Minnow at your service, mum. William Minnow, esquire. Well, not quite yet, but soon, I am certain. And you are?"

Clara blinked. Was this the master of Bleakly Manor? A lanky eel in a suit?

Instant remorse squeezed her chest. Who was she, a woman fallen from the graces of society, to judge the appearance of a man of substance? She dipped her head. "I am Clara Chapman."

"Clara Chapman! Oh, but I like the sound of that." The elder on the chair waved a handkerchief at her. "Step nearer, dearest, and let's look at you up close, shall we?"

Familiar with the idiosyncrasies of the elderly, she complied, but froze several paces in front of the woman. A pink nose with whiskers poked out of the box on the lady's lap, where a hole had been cut jaggedly into the side. Red eyes emerged, followed by a furry body and a naked tail, flesh-coloured and long. A second mouse emerged after it. The two scampered to the edge of the old lady's knee and rose up on hind legs, testing the air with quivering noses.

Clara stiffened. Hopefully the creatures would turn right around and disappear back into the box.

The lady merely scrutinized her as if nothing more than a teacup and saucer rested on her lap. "Such a marvelous creature, Miss Chapman."

Was she speaking of her or the mice? "Th–Thank you," she stuttered. "I am sorry, but I didn't catch your name, ma'am?"

"No, you did not." The lady beamed at her. "I am Miss Scurry, and now we shall all be the jolliest of companions, shall we not?"

"We shall, and more." Mr. Minnow's heels brushed against the carpet, then he reached for her hand and placed it on his arm. "Come, sit and warm yourself, my pet."

Pet? She barely had time to turn the word over before he escorted her to a settee near the hearth and pushed her into it.

"I'm wondering, Miss Chapman"—Mr. Minnow smiled down at

her—"not that Miss Scurry and I aren't exceedingly grateful, for we are, but why exactly have you invited us here to share the Twelve Days with you?"

"Me?" She shook her head, yet the movement did nothing to make sense of his question. "But you are mistaken, for I received an invitation myself."

"Bosh! This is a pickled herring." Flipping out the tails of his suit coat, he joined her on the settee, much too close for propriety. "I thought you, being a lady of such grace and beauty, surely belonged to this house."

"I'm afraid not." She edged away from him.

"Sh-sh-sh." Miss Scurry, evidently just discovering the two escapees had scampered to the top of the box, shooed both mice into the hole on the side and plugged it up with her handkerchief. "Rest, my dears." Then she gazed over at Mr. Minnow. "Don't fret so, my fine fellow. The day of reckoning will come soon enough, and all will be made clear."

Mr. Minnow clapped his hands and rubbed them together. "I suppose there's nothing to be done for it but to wait for the host to appear." His head swiveled, and he narrowed his eyes at Clara. "You're sure that's not you?"

"I am, Mr. Minnow. Very sure."

She bit her lip. Clearly neither of these two eccentrics was the host. So, who was?

CHAPTER FOUR

The prison cart juddered over a hump in the road, rattling Ben's bones. He'd curled into a ball in one corner, tucking his knees to his chest and wrapping his arms about them. Even so, after hours on end and with the chill of night bearing down, there was no stopping the chattering of his teeth. He snorted. Between teeth and bones he was quite the percussionist.

A low "whoa now" slowed the wheels, and finally the cart stopped. Ben jerked upright, crouched and ready, the sudden hammering of his heart forgetting the cold. The long ride here had given him plenty of time to consider his situation, and he'd come to one conclusion—these were his last hours on earth.

So be it. He'd go out fighting against such a wicked injustice and find some measure of worth in the fray.

The scrape of a key shoved into the metal lock, then a click, a creak, and the door swung open. "Yer ride ends here, Lane. Out ye go."

The dark shape of the guard disappeared and light poured in. Ben's eyes watered. Light? Was it day, then? How far had he traveled?

He edged forward, cautious, scanning, as more and more of the world expanded into his view. Black darkened the sky, so it was still night, but torches ablaze changed the immediate area to morning.

"Move along! I've still got a drive back to London." The guard spat out a foul curse. "Ye'd think I'd signed up to be a bleedin' jarvey. They don't pay me enough, I tell ye. Not near enough."

Ben dropped out of the door and immediately wheeled about, fists up, stance wide, prepared for battle.

The guard merely shoved the door shut and relocked it, ignoring him—and there was no one else around.

Truly? No one? Ben stared hard into the darkness beyond the

light. The expansive grounds were rimmed with trees along the perimeter, black against black. Nothing moved except the wind through barren branches. Apparently he'd been taken some distance into the countryside. He turned to face the manor. Impressive, really. Tall. Well masoned. Crenellated at the top. Perhaps used as a stronghold centuries ago.

"Hyah!"

He spun. The cart lumbered down the curved drive, the guard urging the horses onward—without him. He was left standing alone. Unfettered. A brilliant mansion at his back and acres of freedom in front. He could run, here, now. Tear off and flee like the wind. Should he? He scrubbed a hand through his hair, recalling Hacksby's threat.

"You're to be shot on sight for any escape attempt."

The prison cart disappeared into the night. But slowly, emerging out of that same darkness, another shape loomed larger. A carriage, and a fine one at that. Should he wait and meet head-on whomever it carried?

Cold ached in his bare feet and up his legs, yet the pain of the unknown throbbing in his temples hurt worse. He'd have a better chance of putting up a fight if he could actually move his frozen body. Pivoting, he climbed the stairs to the main entrance and rapped the brass knocker.

The door opened immediately, as if the butler had stood behind it waiting for him.

"Welcome, Mr. Lane." The man's upper lip curled to nearly touch his nose.

Ben smirked. He ought be ashamed of his stench, but his time at Millbank had dulled that emotion, especially when it came to issues of hygiene. Even so, he took out his manners and dusted them off. "Thank you. I see you were expecting me."

"Yes, sir. We have a room prepared for you after such a journey. If you would follow me." Turning on his heel, the butler strode the length of the grand foyer toward a door with a stuffed lion head mounted above it.

Ben studied the man as he went. He could pose a threat, for his shoulders were broad as a ceiling beam and those stout legs might pack a wallop of a kick. But the silver streaks in his hair labeled the fellow past his prime. Even so, better to keep his distance.

He followed, leaving plenty of space between them, then paused and stared up at the lion head. Light from the chandelier reflected back brightly from those eyes, transparent, lifelike and—

"Mr. Lane?"

He jumped at the butler's voice. What was wrong with him? There were bigger mysteries afoot than a dead lion. "Of course. Sorry."

He caught up to the man, who'd opened double doors, revealing an even bigger lobby. A wide, carpeted staircase, lit by intermittent wall sconces, led up to a first-floor gallery, where more lamps burned. Interesting that pains had been taken to decorate the outside of the manor, yet not one sprig of holly or mistletoe hung inside.

Behind them, the front door knocker banged. Two stairs ahead of him, the butler stopped and pulled out a gold chain from his waistcoat, then flipped open the lid of a watch tethered to the end of it. His eyebrows pulled into a solid line, and a low rumble in his throat gruffed out. "Pardon me, Mr. Lane. If you'd wait here, please."

Here? On the stairs? A duck at rest to be shot from behind? He waited for the butler to pass, then tracked him on silent feet and slipped into the shadow cast by a massive floor clock.

A man in a sealskin riding cloak entered, frost on his breath and hat pulled low. He stomped his boots on the tiles, irreverent of the peace.

The butler dipped his head. "Mr. Pocket, I presume?"

"I am." The new arrival pulled off his hat and ran a hand through his shorn hair, the top of his head quite the contradiction to his bushy muttonchops. A rumpled dress coat peeked through the gap of his unbuttoned coat, and his trousers looked as if they'd never seen a hot iron. Clearly the man was not married, nor was he the master of the manor.

"You were not due to arrive for another half hour, sir." A scowl tugged down the corners of the butler's mouth.

Mr. Pocket twisted his lips, his great muttonchops going along for the ride. "Yet the invitation did not specify an arrival time, unless. . . ahh! I see. The deliveries were spaced out to ensure a regulated arrival schedule. Am I correct?"

"Very clever, Inspector."

"Part of the job."

So the fellow was a lawman. Ben flattened his back against the wall, sinking deeper into the shadow of the clock. Questions ticked in his mind with each swing of the pendulum. Was Pocket sent to make sure he didn't run or to finish him off? Or possibly set him up for something more sinister than embezzlement and fraud? But why the big charade? Why not just kill him in jail or ship him off as planned?

"If you wouldn't mind stepping in here until dinner, sir." The butler opened a door in a side wall, but his back hindered Ben's view into the room. "You may meet some of the other guests while you wait."

"All right. Don't mind if I do." Mr. Pocket swept past the man and vanished.

Ben dashed back to the stairs, folded his arms, and leaned against the railing as if he'd never moved.

The butler hesitated on the bottom stair only long enough to say, "My apologies for the delay, Mr. Lane. Please, let us continue."

Ben trailed the man as he traveled up two flights, then noted every door they passed and any corridors intersecting the one they traveled. There were two, one lit, one dark. They stopped at the farthest chamber of what he guessed to be the east wing.

The butler opened the door but blocked him from entering. "You'll find a bath drawn in front of the hearth, grooming toiletries on a stand opposite, and a set of dinner clothes laid out on the bed. I shall send a footman up to retrieve you in"—he reclaimed his watch once more and held it up for inspection before tucking it away—"forty-five minutes. Is that sufficient?"

"Very generous," he replied.

"Very good." The butler stepped aside, allowing him to pass, then pulled the door shut.

Ben froze. The chamber gleamed in lamplight and gilt-striped wallpaper, so large and glorious it might overwhelm a duke. At center, a four-poster bed commanded attention, mattresses high enough to require a step stool. Against one wall stood an oversized roll-top desk and matching chair, decked out with full stationery needs. Several padded chairs and three different settees formed two distinct sitting areas. A screen offered privacy for necessary functions, and thick brocaded drapery covered what must be an enormous bank of windows.

He changed his mind. This would overwhelm a king.

Shaking off his stupor, he stalked to the copper basin in front of the fire. Steam rose like a mist on autumn water, smelling of sage and mint. Nine months. Nine never-ending months of filth and sweat and blood.

He stripped off his prison garb, heedless of ripping the threadbare fabric, and kicked the soiled lump from him, uncaring that it lodged beneath the bed. Good riddance.

Water splashed over the rim as he sank into the water, warmth washing over him like a lover's embrace. A sob rose in his throat. This time last year, he'd bathed before dinner just like this. Dressed in fine clothes similar to those laid on the counterpane. Dined by candlelight with the woman he loved fiercely. Kissed Clara's sweet lips until neither of them could breathe.

What a fool.

He snatched the bar of soap off the tray hooked to the tub's side, then scrubbed harder than necessary. Of course this wasn't like last Christmas Eve. It could never be.

For he wouldn't see Clara ever again.

CHAPTER FIVE

Enough was quite enough. Clara rose from the chair and crossed to Miss Scurry's side. Her step faltered only once as she drew near, her distaste of rodents almost getting the better of her, but surely the scrap of handkerchief would keep the mice snug inside the woman's box. Hopefully.

Tears glistened in Miss Scurry's eyes, her quizzing glass dangling forgotten on its ribbon. Clara laid a hand on her shoulder, squeezing a light encouragement. Then she faced Mr. Pocket, who'd stationed himself at the hearth, questioning them all as if they stood before the great white throne.

"Mr. Pocket, I fear your questions are a bit much for Miss Scurry."

"Oh?" The man sniffed, his large nostrils flaring. "Well, perhaps just one more then. Miss Scurry, you say that if you remain the duration of the Twelve Day holiday, your invitation guaranteed the lost would be found, which seems a small thing, depending of course on that which was lost. So tell me, please, what was lost and why is it of such importance? Why weren't you promised money, as in Miss Chapman's case, for then you could replace what was lost? Or if the missing item is not of monetary value, then why not the hope of companionship, a friend, so to speak, which is Mr. Minnow's lure?" Mr. Pocket swept out his hand to where Mr. Minnow primped his cravat in front of a mirror on the other side of the sitting room.

"I. . .I. . ." Miss Scurry stuttered, her words tied on the thread of a whimper. "All will be clear on the day of reckoning."

Clara patted the lady's shoulder. Were all inspectors so bullish? "Mr. Pocket, I believe it is time for you to tell us exactly what *your* invitation stated. It's only fair, and I should think that to a man who upholds justice, fairness is one of your utmost concerns. Is it not?"

A grin stretched the man's lips, from one edge of his long side-burns to the other. "Delightful, Miss Chapman. Were you a man, you'd make a fine inspector." Leaving his post, he strode to a chair adjacent them and sat. "I have nothing to hide, and so I shall state my case plainly. My invitation pledged me a new position. A higher rank. One with more importance."

"And that is?" Clara pressed.

"Magistrate, Miss Chapman. No more slogging through alleys to collar a criminal. No interrogating doxies or cullies or cutthroats. Just a seat on a tall bench with an even taller wig, a blazing hearth fire at my back, and the felons brought to me. Ahh." He closed his eyes, serenity erasing the lines on his brow.

From this angle, lamplight lit some of the shorn hairs on his head with silver. Looking closer, Clara spied the same threads of white sprinkled throughout his sideburns. Her heart softened, imagining the rugged life he'd led roaming the dangerous streets of London. No wonder he wanted to trade professions.

The door opened, interrupting her thoughts and pulling Mr. Pocket to his feet.

"Dinner is served." The butler, resplendent in a black dress coat, matching trousers, and starched white collar, held out his gloved hand in invitation. "If you would all follow me, please."

Mr. Minnow shot to Clara's side, nearly toppling Mr. Pocket as he darted past him. His gingery scent assaulted her nose.

"Allow me to escort you, my pet." He grabbed her hand and placed it on his arm without waiting for an answer.

She gritted her teeth. It was going to be a very long Twelve Days.

They filed out and had just entered the foyer, when the front door burst open and a grey whirlwind blew in, lugging an overstuffed carpetbag and muttering all the way.

"Les idiots! Le monde est rempli des idiots!"

The woman stormed up to the butler and shouted in his face. "Why no one help me carry my bag, eh? Help me from the carriage? Open the door? I will speak to the master of *la maison*. Now!"

Clara blinked. Miss Scurry clutched her box to her chest. Mr. Pocket took a step closer, scrutinizing the interaction.

Yet the butler merely lifted his hand and snapped his fingers.

"Mademoiselle Pretents, I presume?"

"*Oui!*" The short lady stamped her foot.

A footman appeared and, without a word, managed to remove the woman's woolen cape and sweep the bonnet from her head, then collected her bag. The quick movements were so unexpected, even Mademoiselle Pretents stood gaping. Her dark little eyes, which were far too close together, narrowed, following his retreat with her possessions. For half an instant, Clara wondered if she would chase after him like a hound to the kill.

"Let us continue then, shall we?" The butler passed beneath the lion head, the doors now open to reveal a great lobby and a grand stairway.

Mademoiselle Pretents flew across the room, yanking Clara's hand from Mr. Minnow's arm and placing her fingers on his sleeve. "Oui, let us continue."

Clara hid a smile. The woman could have no idea the service she'd just rendered.

The group filed after the butler, Mr. Minnow and Mademoiselle Pretents in the lead, followed by Miss Scurry, then Clara, and finally Mr. Pocket. They passed from elegance to splendor, with gilded-framed portraits decorating the corridor walls and thick Persian runners beneath their feet. The sitting room was a bleak den in comparison. Suddenly it made sense that the master who'd invited them would greet his guests in the dining room, for surely such a great man would want to be seen housed in the finest glory.

"*Très magnifique,*" Mademoiselle Pretents breathed out as she passed through cherrywood doors into the dining room.

"Indeed," Mr. Minnow murmured beside her.

Miss Scurry entered next, then paused and looked over her shoulder at Clara. "Oh, my beauty, it is glorious in here. Come and see."

Crossing the threshold, Clara sucked in a breath. She'd attended some of the finest dinners in London. Danced in many a grand ballroom. Visited and taken tea in posh surroundings. All were slums in comparison.

She entered on cat's feet, padding carefully, unwilling to break the spell of enchantment created by hundreds of crystals raining from chandeliers, lit by candles that must have taken the staff at least a half hour to ignite. Wine-coloured wallpaper, embellished with golden threads, soaked in the light, then reflected it back ever brighter. Silver utensils and fine china adorned the table. Truly, only Buckingham Palace could compare.

At the head of the table, a man stood with his back to them. Tall. Broad of shoulder. Hair the colour of burnt cream, slicked back yet curiously ragged at the ends. Power clung to his frame as finely as his well-tailored dress coat. He belonged here, surrounded by wealth, intimidating any and all who trod weak-kneed into his domain. No one spoke a word. Not even Mademoiselle Pretents.

Clara trembled. Why would such a powerful man invite her here, especially now that she'd sunk so low in society? She was no one.

Slowly, the man turned, gaze passing from person to person. And when those hazel eyes landed on her, she gasped.

A nightmare stared back at her, a ghost from the past who never—ever—should have risen from the grave. The audacity! The gall!

For a moment she froze, gaping, then she shouldered past the other guests and slapped him open-palmed across the face.

CHAPTER SIX

Ben's head jerked aside, the slap echoing in his skull, the crack of flesh upon flesh reverberating in the room. Unbelievable. This whole day had been one big snarl of impossibility. Even more stunning, Clara raised her hand for another strike. The nerve of the little vixen! He grabbed her wrist, unsure who shook more, her or him.

"How dare you invite me here?" Crimson patches of murder stained her cheeks. "And how foolish of me to have walked into your trap. Was my humiliation not enough?"

"*Your* humiliation?" He ground his teeth until his jaw cracked. This was not to be borne. He'd rotted in a gaol cell, been beaten, left cold, hopeless, while this pampered princess suffered what? Dinner parties and suitors in his absence?

She yanked from his grasp, rubbing away his touch. "You are a beast."

A short woman draped in grey and as blustery as a November breeze nudged Clara aside. "I am your servant, *Monsieur*, Mademoiselle Pretents. Shall I dismiss this rabble for you, hmm?" She fluttered her fingertips at Clara.

He frowned. "Surely you're not under the impression that I . . ." He looked past her to the three others inhabiting the dining room. Expectation gleamed in an elderly lady's eyes. Next to her, a thin man's gaze burned with eagerness, and even the muttonchopped inspector, Mr. Pocket, leaned back on his heels in anticipation.

Clara turned and strode to the far side of the table, her body so rigid a carpenter could lay beams across her shoulders.

"Monsieur." The grey lady stepped closer, head bowed. If she were a dog, no doubt her tail would be tucked. "I am so greatly honored to be in your presence."

He stifled a snort—barely. He'd laugh her off, if the situation weren't so brutally ironic. All his life he'd worked hard to achieve status such as this, and now that he was a condemned felon, apparently he had it. A perfectly beautiful paradox, really.

Yet a complete lie. He shook his head. "I am not the master of Bleakly Manor, if that's what you think."

The grey lady's mouth puckered and she spit out a "Pah!" Grabbing handfuls of her skirts, she whirled away.

The inspector edged toward him. "Then who are you, sir?"

"Not that it signifies"—he glanced down the table to where Clara stood, back toward him—"but I am Benjamin Lane."

She did not turn at the name that should've been hers by now, but he did detect a flinch.

"*Lane?* Lane, you say? Hmm." Mr. Pocket stopped in front of him. This close, his magnificent nose took on a whole new proportion, eclipsing the inspector's face. The fellow was nothing but one great beak with side-whiskers. "What were you promised if you stay the duration, Mr. Lane?"

Ben studied him. If the lawman had been sent here to keep an eye on him, then the fellow already knew the answer. But that didn't mean he had to make things easy for the inspector.

"Are you a card player, sir?" Ben asked.

The man's eyes narrowed. "Been known to indulge now and then. Why?"

"Then you will appreciate it when I hold my cards close to my chest."

Mr. Pocket's lips parted to reply, but the butler announced from across the room, "Dinner is served. Please, be seated."

Savory scents entered the room, along with servants bearing all manner of platters and tureens. They lined up their offerings on sideboards against the wall.

Ben waited to see where the odd assortment of guests might land, hoping to distance himself from all and especially from Clara. The betrayer. Unbidden, his gaze slipped to where she sat, near the end of the table. Her beauty goaded. Her raven hair done up in a chignon, loose curls falling to her shoulder, taunted him with memories of when she'd let him nuzzle its silkiness with his cheek—the same cheek that yet stung from her slap.

The thin man sat next to her, far closer than decorum allowed. A footman marched over and bent, whispering into the man's ear. The bony fellow shot up from his chair, upsetting it onto two legs for a moment, then darted to the other side of the table and sank like a kicked puppy onto a different seat.

Only two open seats remained, both next to Clara, one of which was at the head of the table. That gave him only one option, really.

He strode to the seat next to her, the one the bony little man had tried to take, then grimaced to see Benjamin Lane written in gold on the place card. Whoever arranged this meeting was clearly toying with him—with all of them. But to what end?

He grabbed the chair and scooted it as far from her as possible. She inched hers away, as well. Had ever a Christmas Eve been so awkward?

A servant placed bowls of steaming green soup in front of each of them, leastwise what he assumed had been served to all. Hard to tell what went on opposite him now that they were seated. A huge centerpiece, filled with green fronds and peacock feathers, ran the length of the table and blocked his view. But he could hear them. Mademoiselle Pretents's voice berated the server for a perceived slight. The elderly lady cooed about something or maybe to someone. The thin man and the inspector didn't say a word.

Neither did Clara. Nor did she eat. She sat as a Grecian statue, cold, marble, staring into her bowl. Did she even breathe? Not that he cared.

Liar.

He grabbed his spoon and started shoveling in soup. He *did* care, and that's what irked him most. He cared that she'd so easily thrown away everything they'd shared, every laugh, every whisper. Every kiss.

He slammed down the spoon and shoved the bowl away, speaking for her ears alone. "Whatever you may think, I didn't do it."

"I cannot believe you deny what you did." Only her lips moved, for she refused to look at him. Her voice sharpened to a razor edge, one he'd never heard her use before. "You are a thief of the highest order."

Rage coloured the room red. He'd flattened men for lesser insults.

His tone lowered to a growl. "Nor can I believe you so easily accepted such a lie. Tell me, did you lose faith in me immediately after you first heard the accusation, or did you give it a full five minutes?"

She jerked her face to his, blue eyes blazing to violet, the dark kind of purple before a storm. "You are insufferable!"

"I?" Her boldness stole his breath. "Did you even try to find out the truth?"

"What truth? That you put Blythe Shipping out of business? That you ran off with my family's investment? That you've been living like a king God-knows-where while I have been reduced to nothing?" Her chest heaved, and her nostrils flared. A wild mare couldn't have been any more inflamed. "Or are you speaking of the truth wherein you left me standing alone and unwanted at the altar?"

He clenched his hands to keep from throttling her. What nonsense was this? "It's a little hard to attend a wedding—even my own—when locked in a cell at Millbank."

The angry stain on her cheeks bled to white. "Millbank?" she whispered.

Was this a ploy? Some kind of feminine manipulation? He narrowed his eyes. If so, her mistake. He knew her too well, and if her right eye twitched, even the smallest possible tic, her lie would be exposed. "You didn't know?"

"All I know is that you walked out of my life in the worst possible way." A fine sheen of tears shimmered in her gaze, begging for release.

But nothing else. No twitch. No tic. For the first time in nine months, his heart started beating. Perhaps—just maybe—she truly hadn't known he'd been imprisoned. The thought lodged in his mind like a stone, all he'd believed of her swirling around it like water in a river.

By all that was holy, was he falling under her spell yet again? He hardened his resolve and his tone. "On the way to church the morning of our wedding, I was accosted and charged with the embezzlement of Blythe Shipping and your family fortune. I have been at Millbank ever since. Had you the slightest bit of faith in me, you'd have done a little digging and unearthed that nugget of truth."

"This is hardly the garb of an inmate." She swept out her hand. "That suit alone must've cost fifty pounds. Why should I believe you?"

So many emotions waged war; he tugged at his collar, unable to breathe. Whoever had indicted him had not only stolen his freedom, but the good opinion of the only woman he'd ever cared about. Blowing out a sigh, he edged his chair nearer to her. "Look closer, Clara. Look beyond what you think you know to what really is."

Her gaze traveled over his face, pausing on leftover bruises, widening at recent scars, and finally landing on the bump on his nose caused by one too many breaks. For a moment, the tears in her eyes threatened to spill, and then a hard glaze turned them to glass. "For all I know, you've been brawling over some gambling debt. Tell me, have you lost everything you've taken so soon?"

"I did not do it!" He growled like the beast she'd claimed him to be.

At the opposite end of the table, the inspector stood. "Everything all right down there, Miss Chapman?"

"Don't concern yourself on my behalf, Mr. Pocket." She glared at Ben and lowered her voice. "No one else has."

He gaped. He'd taken a punch in the lungs before, but never something as breath stealing as this. He shoved back his chair and stood, done with dinner before the main course and definitely done with Clara Chapman.

"Oh flap! Oy me rumpus! Who's the wiggity scupper what called me here? Watch yer driving, Jilly." A wheeled chair barreled through the dining room doors, pushed by a slip of a girl. She shoved the chair to the head of the table, jiggling a large toad of a man seated atop, until both came to a stop. Everyone's wineglasses quivered from the impact.

The fellow grumbled as if he were the one being inconvenienced. "Now that I'm here, whyn't we just pay me debt straight off and drink away the rest o' the days? Which one of you guppers holds the money bags, eh?"

Murmurs circled the table.

The butler once again entered from a far door. "Ahh, Mr. Tallgrass. A bit tardy, but we are pleased you have joined us."

"Oh flap! Oy me rumpus! Jilly, lend a hand."

The girl, face drawn into a perpetual sulk, left her post at the back of his chair and grabbed ahold of the front of his shirt, yanking him upward. Then just like that, she let go, so that he flopped backward, now straightened, with a huge sigh.

His head swiveled to Clara. "Well, here's a fine tablemate. I likes the look o' you, I do."

Ignoring them all, Ben stalked away from the macabre gathering and took the stairs two at a time. Australia would've been better than this.

The Second Day

DECEMBER 25, 1850

Chapter Seven

Clara startled awake, heart pounding. Bed sheets tangled around her legs, and she clutched the counterpane to her neck. Grey light slipped in through the drawn draperies where they didn't quite meet. Not fully morning, but it would do. She'd tossed and turned enough to call it a night, waking from every dream, each one a variation of Ben's face. Of the hurt in his eyes. The wildness. The pain creasing his brow. If she listened hard enough, she might yet hear the haunting echo of the anguish in his voice.

"I did not do it!"

She knotted the sheet in her hands. What if he spoke true? His pale skin had lacked his usual healthy luster. A fresh scrape had marred the temple near his left eye, a new crescent scar cut across his jaw, and his once straight nose was now aquiline. Not to mention the stark bones defining his cheeks, testifying to a lack of nutrition. All lent credence to his claim of being locked in Millbank. It wasn't a huge leap of faith to change her belief that indeed he'd not run off to Europe with embezzled funds—but that merely meant he'd been caught beforehand. Didn't it?

So why would her brother, George, allow her to believe otherwise?

She shoved the counterpane aside and sat up. Why indeed. She lifted her face to the ceiling, breathing out the prayer that was now as much a part of her as flesh and bone.

Why, God? Why?

Snatching her wrap from the end of the mattress, she shivered into it. The fire in the hearth had long since died out. Good thing she'd kept her stockings on. Hopefully Aunt would not venture from her bed on this chill of a Christmas morn.

Clara dressed in the semilight, unwilling to lose any warmth to the windows until fully clothed, then she pulled the draperies wide and gasped. La! Such a view. A walled garden coated with a light dusting of snow lay just beneath her wing of the building. Beyond that, rolling hills and, farther on, a wood with towering trees. How lovely this would be when spring blew green upon it.

But for now, wind rattled the panes. Cold air snaked in through a gap in the caulk, and she retreated a step, feeling the chill beneath the grandeur. Both the manor and the grounds were beautiful, yet she could not shake the morbid feeling the place was somewhat of a sham.

Turning away from the scene, she settled in front of a small dressing table and set about pinning up her hair. Winter or not, Ben or not, she would celebrate this Christmas morn, leastwise in spirit, in memory of the Babe sent to atone for all.

She shoved in the last pin just as a small envelope was thrust beneath her chamber door. What on earth? Rising from the chair, she crossed the rug to retrieve it. The thick envelope weighed heavy in her palm, definitely denser than the invitation of yesterday. Would each day bring a new set of instructions, then?

Breaking the seal, she opened the flap, then shook out a single gold coin. Nothing else. No note. No directions. She held the coin up, catching the light from the window. Jagged edges detracted from what used to be a perfect circle. On one side, letters too worn to be read ringed around a raised X. No, wait. Maybe it was a cross. Hard to tell. She flipped it over. An ornate twining of embellishment encircled two words:

Secundus Casus

"*Secundus casus*," she whispered, but even voicing the words aloud didn't make any sense of them. Absently, she rubbed her thumb over the engraving, a sinking feeling settling low in her stomach. If her assumption was right, the message was in Latin—a language Ben had studied as a boy. Did she care enough about this mystery to ask him for his help in translation?

She tapped a finger to her lips. Did it matter what the thing said? Perhaps the coin was a simple gift, given to everyone by the master of the house, a master they'd meet at breakfast. Surely that must be it. Tucking the coin into her pocket, she smoothed her skirts, then opened the door, prepared to meet the host who had called them here.

Indeed, this would be a day of answers and—

A scream violated the sanctity of Christmas morning. She froze, hand still on the knob, and debated if she ought turn back and lock herself in.

Farther down the hall, another door opened, and Miss Scurry, toting her box, darted out. Her frantic steps swirled the hem of her skirt around her ankles. "Oh! Dear me!" She jerked her face toward Clara, the quizzing glass pinned to her bodice swinging with the movement. "Dear you! Are you quite all right, Miss Chapman?"

"It wasn't me." She sped to the old lady's side, offering an arm in case she swooned.

Footsteps pounded down the stairs, and three men bolted toward them, Ben in the lead, followed by Mr. Pocket, and finally Mr. Minnow.

Breathless, cravat yet untied, Ben stopped in front of them. "What's happened?"

Biting her lip, Clara shook her head, unsure how to answer.

He slid his gaze to Miss Scurry. "Are you ill, madam?"

"Such a dear. Such a gentleman." Miss Scurry beamed up at him. "I am well, sir."

But the next scream indicated someone else was not.

Chapter Eight

Ben wheeled about and sprinted down the hall, the inspector at his side. Retracing their route past the staircase, they bolted into a different corridor. Halfway down, a door stood ajar. Heated words raged within, a woman's voice calling down brimstone upon some unfortunate soul.

Slowing, Ben glanced at the inspector, who had his gun drawn. Unarmed, Ben wouldn't be much help to the man. Their gazes met for an instant, and Pocket gave a single nod of understanding, then took the lead.

The inspector shoved the door open and barreled into the chamber. "Halt! Whatever's afoot, be done with it!"

Ben stationed himself at the threshold, prepared to collar a fleeing rogue if necessary. But the room was empty, save for the grey lady, Mademoiselle Pretents.

The woman spun, brows pinched low enough to hood her eyes. "Oui, monsieur! Such villainy must be stopped."

The inspector swiveled his head, scanning the room, then loosened the hammer on his pistol and tucked it away. "What has you in such a state, mademoiselle? Are you unwell?"

"No! I am not well." Her fists popped onto her hips. A ruffled peahen couldn't have puffed up nearly as much. "There is a thief at loose. My jewels have been stolen. All of them!"

Ben advanced and studied the room. The windows were shut tight. There were no adjoining doors to this chamber. All was tidy, even the bed, as if the woman had slept atop the counterpane, for surely such a firebrand would not deign to make up the bedclothes herself.

"Now, now, miss." The inspector pulled out a chair from a nearby dressing table. "Why don't you sit yourself down and tell me all about it?"

"No! I will not sit. I will not rest. Not until my jewels are returned." She stamped her foot, and the inspector retreated a step.

Ben sighed. Some Christmas morning this was turning out to be. "Mr. Pocket can't help you if you don't tell him exactly what happened, madam."

Were he a superstitious man, he'd motion the sign of the cross to ward off the evil eye she shot him. Yet she lifted her skirts and settled on the chair.

Pocket dragged over a cushioned stool and sat in front of her. "All right, then, let's have it."

"Before I went to bed last night, I hid my pouch—a velvet one, black—inside my chamber pot, for who would think to look there, no? I rose early, before any maid could come take it away, and *voila.*" Her arm shot out, and she pointed to a porcelain urn next to the bed. "Empty!"

Rising, both he and the inspector crossed to the pot and peered in. Only a hairline crack at the bottom stared up at them.

Pocket turned back to the woman, his chest expanding with a deep breath. Ben hid a smile. The woman likely had no idea the interrogation that was about to rain down upon her head.

"What was in the pouch?" the inspector asked.

"My jewels."

"Yes, you've said that. What kind, exactly?"

"Valuable ones."

"Details, mademoiselle." The inspector cocked his head. "Details, please."

"A necklace, a bracelet, and a ring. All gold."

"The stones?"

"Diamonds, so glittery."

"The chain?"

"As I have said, gold."

"Single? Twisted? Any kind of pattern?"

The woman glowered.

The inspector leaned toward her. "Family heirloom?"

"Of course!"

"Whose?"

Clearly rattled, the woman sank against the chair. Ben smirked.

The inspector had fired out his questions so quickly, she'd not had time to speak anything but the truth. Yet it wasn't so much what she said, but what she didn't say, a trick he'd learned after suffering one too many examinations himself.

A curious transformation took place. Instead of tears or even a whimper, the grey lady shot to her feet and clenched her hands. Red crept up her neck and bloomed on her cheeks. "Why you question me when it is my jewels that have been stolen, eh?"

Interesting. Anger combined with a lack of minute description of her goods? And no grief whatsoever about the family connection to the jewels? Ben studied her set jaw and glittering black eyes. Perhaps the woman wasn't the original owner of the trinkets but had stolen them herself.

"Oh, dear. Oh, my!" The words cooed from behind.

Ben glanced back to the door. The thin man, the elderly lady, and Clara all stood, eyes wide.

"Out! Out! All of you." The grey woman threw out her hands, and Ben had no doubt she'd shoo them off like a murder of crows. "Go! I will manage this on my own."

"Then you shouldn't have screamed in the first place, madam," the inspector grumbled as he passed by Ben. "Nevertheless, I will see what can be done to find your jewels."

Before Clara turned to tread down the hallway, Ben caught a glimpse of her face. Skin pale. Curved shadows beneath each eye. Her shoulders drooped and her step lagged. Apparently she'd not slept. A yawn overtook him as he followed the group to the top of the stairs. Neither had he, despite the comfort of a feather mattress instead of a cold stone floor. This should have been the first Christmas shared with his wife—as one flesh. Whoever stole that from him and poisoned Clara's mind against him would pay. He clenched the handrail so tightly, his fingers ached.

The inspector led the pack, followed by the thin man, Mr. Minnow, who pelted Pocket's back with questions. Miss Scurry clutched her box with one hand and the railing with the other. Clara hovered behind her. Ben brought up the rear, mulling over the quirky behavior of all the guests, Mademoiselle Pretents foremost. Whether the jewels were hers or not, the fact remained that a thief roamed this manor, one bold enough to enter a woman's chamber in the middle of the night and steal. And if this one had no qualms at such flagrant behaviour, what other devious acts might the villain stoop to?

At the bottom of the stairs, Ben sprang ahead. No matter what Clara thought of him—or he of her—he would not allow her safety to be compromised. "Clara," he whispered, reluctant to draw the attention of the others.

She glanced at him but did not stop.

"Please, a word."

Her mouth flattened into a line, but she complied, stopping near the clock where he'd hidden in the shadow the night before.

He drew near, abhorring how her rosewater scent made his pulse quicken. A stranger stared back at him. He hated that love and hope and a life together had been ripped out from beneath them both. But most of all, he hated whoever had been responsible for the confusion and hurt wounding Clara's gaze. Of all the things he wanted to say, wanted to know, he simply said, "Be sure to keep your door locked whenever you're in your chamber."

Chapter Nine

Clara slipped past Ben, escaping as much from his concern as her confusion. Oh, for the days when everything made sense and the world ran in perfect order. A groan lodged in her throat. Convict or not, Ben made it impossible for her to think straight when he was standing but a breath away. His direct gaze unnerved her with an untamed light she'd never before seen. Surely he hadn't been the one to steal the woman's jewels. Had he? She hurried along the hallway, swiping a loosened strand of hair from her eyes along with the question.

Mr. Minnow pounced the moment her toe crossed the dining-room threshold. "Over here, Miss Chapman." His fingers wrapped around her upper arm, and he tugged her to an empty chair next to his. "I shall plate you the tastiest morsels, my pet. Don't trouble yourself to move an inch."

She covered a grimace with what she hoped came off as a small smile. As much as she'd disliked the arranged seating of last night's dinner, was this truly any better? "Perhaps we ought wait, Mr. Minnow, until the master of the house arrives."

But her words were too late to stop him. He already stood at the sideboard.

Next to her, a dish landed on the table and Mr. Pocket sank onto the chair with a huff. "Curious choice of fare, I'd say."

An odd aroma—a mixture of jasmine and headcheese—wrinkled her nose. She peeked at the man's meal. His fork prodded a mound of brownish gelatin, each poke bleeding out colourless liquid. Lemon slices added stripes of yellow to the lump. This was breakfast?

"A curious morning, to be sure." She pulled her gaze from his plate. "Do you know who's taken Mademoiselle Pretents's jewels, Inspector?"

"That I do not, miss, but don't fret. I shall figure it out, sooner or later. Guilt has a way of coming to light no matter what dark corner it tries to hide in. All the same, be sure to lock your door at night." He shoveled in a big bite, and she turned from the sight, unwilling to watch it travel down his throat.

She reached for the tea urn as Ben entered the room and Mr. Minnow graced her with a plate of the quivering aspic. "Thank you, sir."

Mr. Minnow drew himself up a full six inches at her gratitude.

"Oh flap! Oy me rumpus!" Mr. Tallgrass rolled in, his wheeled chair crashing into the table with such force it bounced him backward. "Jilly, lend a hand," he rumbled.

The dark-haired waif—how could one so thin push about such a great toad?—dashed to his side and yanked him upward, then let go. The wind punched from his lungs in a cough, but then a churlish grin rippled across his lips.

Ben took a seat at the far end of the table, which for some reason irked Clara, but before she could think to dissect such a feeling, the butler filled the doorway and rang a bell, drawing all their eyes—except for Mr. Tallgrass.

"Turn me about, Jilly!" He snaked out his hand and cuffed the girl on the head. "Poxy rag-a-ma-tag."

Setting down the small bell, the butler struck such a pose that Clara couldn't help but wonder if he'd served in the military. "Excuse me, ladies and gentlemen, but your gracious host—"

"And who would that be?" Mr. Minnow leaned forward in his seat.

The butler rocked on his heels. "I am instructed to inform you all that while your invitations stand as is, there is a recent addendum. Only one of you will receive a reward for staying the duration of the twelve nights."

"Who, dear? Which one?" Miss Scurry's voice squeaked. Or was that one of her mice?

"The one who remains."

Mr. Pocket angled his head at Clara. "Rather cryptic, eh miss?"

"Indeed," she whispered.

The butler cleared his throat. "Christmas dinner shall be served promptly at 7:00 p.m." His dark eyes shot to Mr. Tallgrass for a moment. "Charades will follow in the drawing room, with a basket of prepared scenarios that will be atop the pianoforte."

"Rather explicit instructions for so early in the day. I take it you will not be in attendance?" asked Mr. Pocket.

"Another astute observation, Inspector. You are correct. I shall be leaving the premises after breakfast."

Miss Scurry murmured an "oh dear," but the butler went right on with his last words. "As you all may have noticed, the outside of Bleakly Manor has been properly decorated for the Twelfth Night festivities. The inside, however, requires Christmas decor. I've been given a list of assignments you are expected to accomplish before dinner tonight."

He pulled out a small slip of paper from an inside pocket. "Mr. Minnow, you are paired with Mademoiselle Pretents, as soon as she makes an appearance."

Mr. Minnow's lower lip quivered, and he spoke so only Clara might hear. "I'd so hoped to be with you, my pet."

The butler narrowed his eyes at him. "The two of you will hang the mistletoe and drape the ivy." His gaze returned to the instructions. "Mr. Pocket will aid Miss Scurry—"

"Oh!" Miss Scurry fluttered her free hand to her chest. "But I'd hoped to be with Mr. Minnow. Such a kind man."

Once again, the butler continued as if nothing had been said. "You are to decorate the Christmas tree, which is placed on a table in the drawing room. Mr. Tallgrass and his assistant, Miss Jilly, shall—"

"Oh flap! Yer not sticking me with grunt work what ought be done by some kiddly-wugget of a slackin' servant." Mr. Tallgrass's cheeks puffed out, his skin mottling to a deep red. " 'Tain't right! 'Tain't fair! 'Tain't—"

"Mr. Tallgrass!" The butler's voice thundered. "Pay attention, if you please."

"No, I don't very well please," he shot back. "This is a load o' horse droppings!"

The butler's brow creased, and he bent at eye level with the man. "Then you may leave now, if you wish."

Mr. Tallgrass's stubbly whiskers stuck out like white porcupine quills, so tightly did his face squinch up.

The butler straightened as he explained their task, but Clara's thoughts snarled. That only left—

"Mr. Lane, you shall escort Miss Chapman on an outing to retrieve the Yule log for the holiday. You'll find all you should need in the carriage house."

The butler droned on, but his words faded to gibberish. She was to spend the whole of the morning outside with Ben? The man who may—or in his words may not have—caused her and her family so much grief. This was too much to be borne!

Pressing two fingers to her temple, she rubbed little circles to ward off the birth of a headache. She should leave. Now. Just pack up and go home to Aunt.

Spending Christmas, or any other day, with Ben—alone—was the last thing she wanted to do.

Chapter Ten

Frigid air slapped Clara on the cheek, and she tucked her chin to her chest, warding off further assault. On the far side of the wagon seat, Ben snapped the reins, urging the horses onward. Once they reached the shelter of the woods, the wind wouldn't attack with such a wicked sting. But here, on the expanse of rolling hills between manor and forest, the cold was relentless.

So were the warring emotions battling inside her. Anger. Confusion. Doubt and indignation. It was a wicked jest to have been paired up with Ben, and when the master of Bleakly Manor finally showed his face, she'd have a word or two—no, three or more—to share with the man.

"Move closer." Ben glanced at her sideways, face unreadable. "I vow I won't pick your pockets."

"I'm f–fine." Brilliant. Her chattering teeth branded her a fraud. Not that it should matter, for one fraud ought abide with another, should he not?

"Whoa." Ben eased the horses to a halt.

She wrapped her arms tighter and lifted her face. They were hardly near the woods or the house. "What are you doing?"

Shrugging out of his coat, he reached for her with one arm and pulled her toward him. He tucked the wool around her shoulders, then settled her at his side. Leftover heat from his body penetrated her cloak, warming her in ways that went beyond such a generous deed. He grasped the reins and started the horses moving again, the weight of his coat hugging her like an intimate embrace—one that irked and soothed at the same time.

The wagon rambled on, his big arm jostling next to her, his thigh bumping against hers. Hard to tell what made him shudder.

The uneven ground? Guilt? Or the thinness of his dress coat against the bitter air?

"Please, take back your coat." She started to peel it off. "You'll catch your death."

His hand caught hers, gently forcing it to her lap. "Isn't that what you want?"

She frowned up at him. "No, I do not wish you ill."

She wished him to be gone.

A tense silence followed, and her heart ached for the way things had been, when she'd believed in his integrity and was for once in her life sure of love. This Ben, this stranger with the clenched jaw and stiff shoulders, was a shocking replacement.

"I am sorry. My manners are not as pretty as they once were." Pulling his attention from the horses, he gazed down at her. "Are you feeling warmer?"

"Yes, though I insist you take back your coat as soon as we stop."

"Trust me. I've suffered worse than cold." A half smile lifted his lips.

He pulled the wagon to a stop at the edge of the woods, then hopped down and circled to offer her a hand. As soon as her feet hit the ground, she removed his coat and held it out.

He shook his head. "Stubborn as ever, I see."

"I insist. Besides, I am much warmer now that we are more sheltered."

While he shoved his arms back into his coat and buttoned up, she studied the unending maze of tree trunks. Better that than dwell on all the what-might-have-beens that Ben's presence unearthed.

"So, now what?" she asked.

Ben stared into the woods, the sullen sky as clouded as his expression. "Try to spy a large piece of downed wood. Then I'll loosen a horse and retrieve it. We may end up doing this again, for I doubt we'll be able to load a log large enough to last the entire Yuletide."

He stalked ahead, his long legs eating up the ground. She did double time behind him in a vain attempt to keep up—until he glanced over his shoulder and saw her predicament.

A sheepish smile quirked his mouth, and he stopped. "Forgive me. I've not had the pleasure to hike free in so long that I've gotten carried away. This pace is far too fast for you."

He waited while she caught up, and she offered him a wry smile in return. "I'd like to see you try tromping through the frozen woods in petticoats."

He grunted. "No doubt."

Side by side, they advanced, scouring the ground for a fallen tree weathered enough to burn well. Other than the whoosh of wind rattling the branches up high, they walked in companionable silence. Too companionable. How could a thief walk so carefree next to the one he supposedly robbed? The incongruity of it all shivered across her shoulders.

Her step faltered, and Ben grabbed her elbow, righting her. Would that the grief and sorrow of the past nine months could be as easily righted.

"Oh, very well!" She spoke as much to herself as to him, frustrated with the whole situation. She stopped and peered up at him. "I am ready to hear what happened to you and how you came to Bleakly Manor."

"Are you?" His amber gaze held her for a moment. So many emotions shone in those depths. It would take years to sort them all by name. Time froze, the space between them brittle and sharp as the cold air.

Then he wheeled about and strode ahead, pausing only long enough to hold back a low-lying branch for her to pass beneath. Stubborn man!

She grabbed his sleeve before he could pass her again. "Please, Ben."

He blew out a puff of frozen mist, a slight shake to his head. "It is nothing different than what I told you last night. I was on my way to the church, speeding, actually, for such was my eagerness to make you mine, when a gaol cart pulled in front of me, blocking my path. So focused was I on the impediment, I did not notice the men behind me." His voice lowered, yet gained in strength. "I was bagged without seeing who attacked. I awoke two days later in Millbank, where I've been rotting ever since, until I received an invitation to Bleakly Manor, promising me freedom. Freedom." A bitter chuckle rent the cold air. "I no longer believe in such."

He stomped ahead, apparently finished with the conversation.

But she wasn't. Gathering her skirts, she darted after him. "Are you saying you were held without representation? Without bail?"

He snorted. "Often without food or water."

The fine hairs at the back of her neck prickled. If what he said was true...

She hugged herself tightly, as an image of him deprived of nourishment, robbed of dignity, quaked through her, more unsettling than the cold.

She hastened her steps to catch up to him. "I find it hard to believe the justice system could fail on such a grand level. Did you have no trial whatsoever?"

"Oh, I had a trial. At least in word. But my accuser never appeared, sending a proxy instead. The documents remained sealed and unread. As was the evidence. I have no idea who indicted me of the embezzlement of Blythe Shipping or your family fortune." His hands curled into fists at his side. "I was sentenced to transportation before year's end."

Her jaw dropped. Banishment without due process? Unheard of. Wasn't it? "How can that be? Surely that is not how our courts function."

His feet hit the ground harder than necessary, grinding sticks and frozen brush beneath his step. "Enough money can make anything happen. Anything."

His words swirled over her head, as ominous as the darkening clouds pregnant with a winter storm. How was she to understand that? "Are you saying someone bribed the judge to convict you for a crime of which you were innocent?"

He wheeled about before she finished the question. In two strides, he gripped her arms and pulled her close, his voice deadly quiet. "Look me in the eyes, Clara, and tell me you believe I am guilty."

Desperation roughened his tone, harsh and dreadful, compelling her to obey. Never had he used such severity with her.

Swallowing the tightness in her throat, she slowly met his gaze, fearful yet strangely eager to discover the truth. Would she find healing or damnation?

She stared deeply, beyond the golden flecks in his hazel eyes. The purity she saw there flattened the house of cards she'd carefully constructed over the past months. Oh how much easier it would be to cling to the belief that he was a vile cullion. But God help her, she could not.

"No—" Her voice broke, and she sucked in a shaky breath. "I do not believe you are guilty."

A groan rumbled in his chest, and he closed his eyes. "Thank God."

"But. . ." Who had done this? Stolen his freedom? Robbed them of happiness? The world turned watery, and hot tears burned down her face. "I don't understand."

He pulled her into his arms, wrapping her tight against him, and she wept into his shirt. Oh, how she'd missed this. His heart beat hard against her cheek, and she clutched his back, burrowing closer. How good, how right it felt to be in his arms again, share his warmth, lose herself in his comfort. For one glorious moment, she dared surrender to the feeling of being wanted and cherished.

Too soon he broke the embrace. He stepped back and tilted her chin up with the crook of his knuckle. "I should like to hear why you suspected me of such a heinous crime."

A familiar ache throbbed in the thin space between heart and soul—the empty hollow where she stored all her hurt, carved out long ago by her father and his rejection. To speak it aloud would only breathe life into that pain. Love, once poured out, could never go back into the same bottle.

But how could she refuse the earnest expectation on Ben's face? He looked like a lost little boy, abandoned and forlorn. She didn't think it possible, but one more piece of her heart broke off, leaving a jagged edge in her chest.

He reached for her hand. "Perhaps it will be easier if we carry on with our search, hmm?"

Side by side, they pressed on, and he was right. Without facing him the words came easier. "I stood alone that day. Waiting for you to come. The eyes of God and those gathered alternated between me and the front door. At first I suspected the worst had become of you. Some accident or illness, perhaps. I searched every hospital. Inquired with physicians and surgeons. I even sent a servant to visit the morgue. It wasn't until a week later that I learned the truth. Or thought I did."

She paused to step over a snow-dusted rock. "George was summoned to the solicitor's and told the bulk of our family investments—along with Blythe Shipping's—had been stolen. By you."

She studied him from the corner of her eye, expecting some kind of outburst. None came.

"From that day forward," she continued, "we lived just above poverty. Great Aunt Mitchell took me in as her companion, and George sailed for America, hoping to find a living large enough to pay for my fare. In the meantime, I've learned sewing skills beyond mere ornamentation. I intend to earn my keep by soliciting a mending and tailoring service once he sends for me."

For a long time, Ben said nothing, just kept stalking through the frozen woods until he stopped in front of a tree trunk long since fallen. Squatting, he rubbed his hands together, then brushed off the top coating of snow from the wood. "This will do."

He rose and faced her, blowing warmth into his hands. "Think carefully, Clara. Are you certain that meeting between George and the solicitor took place a full week *after* I had been arrested, and that your standard of living didn't alter until then?"

"That's right."

"Hmm." A muscle jumped on his jaw, a sure sign his mind raced.

"What?"

"I am wondering how I could have taken the money, yet it didn't disappear until long after I'd been gaoled?" The question hung between them, icy and bitter as the winter wind, and she trembled at the flatness in his voice.

For the first time, she began to fathom he'd been wronged every bit as much as she—or more. "Who would do such a thing?" she whispered.

"I don't know." His face hardened, the dark gleam in his eyes fearsome. "But I intend to find out."

CHAPTER ELEVEN

A monster rumbled inside Ben's gut, clawing and angry. A familiar feeling, this hunger. He shifted on the settee. Maybe the movement would stop the grumbling, for the odd Christmas dinner they'd eaten this evening certainly hadn't. There'd been no goose or chestnut stuffing. No pâtés or oysters or puddings. Just a plain bouillon, followed by a single roasted Cornish hen and mince pie for the eight of them. No doubt if he listened hard enough, he'd hear echoing growls from the stomachs of those gathered in the drawing room.

Rubbing his fingers together, he stared at the ink stains that would not disappear, though he'd scrubbed hard enough in the basin. After retrieving the Yule log with Clara, he'd spent the afternoon at the desk in his chamber. When he received the promised freedom by Twelfth Night—*if* he did—he'd still need his family wealth reinstated. Money once taken by the Crown was not easily gained back, but it could be done. Ten letters to various officials had left his fingers cramped. If even one of those missives made it into the hands of a sympathetic ear, he'd gladly endure the blackened skin. And with the hope of justice, he'd do the same on the morrow.

In the center of the room, Mr. Minnow flapped about, then fell and curled into a ball.

"Oh, dear! Such wonderful dramatics." Miss Scurry grasped her box of mice close to her chest. "Are you a goose, Mr. Minnow? Taken down by an arrow?"

The man uncurled long enough to touch his nose, then he smiled at Clara. Whether she ventured a guess or not, he always sought her out. The unwarranted attention annoyed Ben as much as his empty belly.

"So, the second word is *goose*, eh?" The inspector sniffed, his nose rubbed raw from having to touch it so many times for when he'd performed his charade, such was the length of "God Rest Ye Merry Gentlemen, Let Nothing You Dismay."

Next to him, Clara leaned near, speaking for Ben alone. "I daresay neither of us expected to be playing games with strangers this Christmas Day, though I fear Mr. Minnow thinks of himself as our bosom companion."

Ben hid a smirk. The man wanted to be her companion, not his.

Clara's gaze followed the game, his traveled the room. The great log burned in the hearth. It wouldn't last the whole of the twelve days, which had set off a superstitious flutter from Miss Scurry, but for now the flames were merry. Ivy swagged over the doors, a little crooked, but if he'd had to work with Mademoiselle Pretents, he'd have made haste in hanging the greenery, as well. For tonight, the Christmas tree on the table glowed with candles attached by clips to the branches. A single servant, an odd little woman, stood nearby with a bucket of water should a fire break out.

A round of applause ended his surveillance. Minnow flopped a bow, then retrieved a basket from the pianoforte and delivered it to Ben.

He shook his head. "I am content to watch. My playacting skills leave much to be desired."

"Oh, but you must." The tang of ginger traveled on the man's words. Minnow shoved the basket into Ben's hands. "There's one in here for each of us."

Scowling, he pulled out an envelope with his name penned on the front. How had Mr. Tallgrass managed to escape this fate? Truth be told, though, Ben's spirits had lightened when the toady fellow rolled off after dinner with a curse about the food and something about the queen.

Clara peered up at him. Lamplight sparkled in her eyes, and—dare he hope—a renewed spark of trust in him, as small as it may be. Even so, this was not the carefree woman he'd known before, not with that buried layer of hurt dulling her gaze. A familiar rage coursed through his veins, heating him from the inside out. He would discover who'd caused this pain, for him and for her, or die in the trying.

"You saw what a poor charade I rendered." She smiled. "You can do no worse."

He snorted. She had no idea.

"Oui. The woman speaks true." Mademoiselle Pretents left her perch on a chair near the hearth and sat nearer the door, face flushed.

Ben rose, and Minnow immediately took his spot, sinking next to Clara. No wonder the fellow had chosen him next.

Resigned to death by humiliation, he crossed to the middle of the room and opened the envelope, but the words made little sense. Thus far, all the charades were related by a holiday theme. Not this. Still, it should be easy enough to perform. He tucked the envelope into his pocket and pretended to pull out a gold piece, holding up the imaginary coin then pantomiming a test of it with his teeth.

"A farthing?" asked Mr. Minnow.

Miss Scurry held up her quizzing glass to one eye and strained forward in her seat. "A sovereign?"

"A gold sovereign?" Clara wondered.

Ben shook his head. This would be harder than he thought. How else to show a—

"Coin!" The inspector shouted.

Ben tapped his nose then held up three fingers.

The inspector nodded. "The third word is *coin*."

He tapped his nose again. Now, how to playact the first two? He froze, the weight of all eyes squashing the life out of his creativity. Or maybe it wasn't the guests' gazes at all. He spun, certain someone watched him from behind. Nothing but the eyes of the portraits on the walls stared back.

"A spinning top?" Mr. Minnow ventured.

"No, a whirligig, you stupid fellow." Mademoiselle Pretents's voice was venom.

Ben wheeled about, shaking his head. The sooner this was over with, the better, but should he act out the only idea Clara was sure to guess? Sucking in a breath, he crossed over to her and dropped to one knee, taking her hand in his.

Colour flamed on her cheeks, and her fingers trembled. Clearly she understood his meaning.

"Proposal!" Minnow aimed the word at him like a dagger to the heart.

Without pulling his gaze from Clara, he shook his head. Slowly, he rubbed his thumb over her third finger, just below the knuckle—the skin now naked where she'd once worn his ring. Dredging up all the memories of passion and whispers they'd shared, he lowered his carefully constructed mask, and allowed a forgotten desire to soften the hard lines on his face.

"Oh, lovely!" Miss Scurry twittered.

Clara gasped.

But playacting a second chance of asking for her hand turned sour at the back of his throat. Why had he ever thought to do such a thing? He shot to his feet and stalked to the hearth, done with the whole charade.

"Love is a two-sided coin?" the inspector guessed. "Oh, I get it. Two-sided coin, eh?"

Ben yanked out the envelope and tossed it into the flames, watched for a moment until fire caught hold of the three words, then spun and touched his nose.

A lie, but so be it.

The Third Day

DECEMBER 26, 1850

CHAPTER TWELVE

E arly morning light hung like a haze in Clara's chamber. Yawning, she rubbed her eyes, and a terrific growl rumbled in her belly. Hopefully today's breakfast would be more palatable than last evening's Christmas dinner.

She threw off the counterpane and snatched her dressing gown from the foot of the bed, heart sinking into her empty stomach. If the burnt smell on the air was any indication, there wasn't much hope of a hearty meal today, either.

Stretching a kink out of her neck, she silently thanked God for tea, for therein she might wake fully and fill her—

"Fire!"

A woman's cry came from below. Danger thudded a crazed beat in Clara's ears. No, were those footsteps? She shot to the door and darted into the hall. A foggy blur softened the edges of everything as she raced to the stairs. Ahead, Ben, Mr. Minnow, and Mr. Pocket surged down the steps, taking several at a time, nightshirts flapping untucked from their trousers. She followed.

At the landing, the men split. Mr. Minnow and Mr. Pocket veered right. Ben headed left. By the time she descended, Ben shouted, "Over here!"

They converged upon the drawing room, where Miss Scurry stood outside the door, wringing her hands. Her usual box of mice was absent. Inside the room, charcoal clouds billowed near the ceiling, pushed upward by flames on the Christmas tree burning at the far corner of the room.

Miss Scurry turned to Clara, fear leaking down her cheeks. "Oh dear! Oh my."

"The drapery, men! Haul to!" Ben no sooner issued his command than he faced Clara. "We'll try to smother it, but seek water just in case. Miss Scurry, check on Mademoiselle Pretents, if you please."

Ben tore into the room, leaving them in the hall with smoke and dread.

Next to her, Miss Scurry whimpered. "The reckoning. Oh! The reckoning is upon us."

Clara reached for the older lady's hand and gave it a squeeze. "All will be well. I am sure the men will smother the flames. We must do as Ben says."

A wavery smile rippled across the old lady's lips. "Such a dear." Then she whirled and fled down the hall, skirts flying behind.

Clara hurried the other way. Why had the old lady dressed so early? And why venture to the drawing room when surely her stomach was as empty as theirs? The dining room made more sense to seek out.

But there was no time to ponder such things. There must be a doorway nearby to a stair leading down to the kitchen, perhaps disguised as mere paneling, for only servants would use it. She studied the wall as she went, disliking the way all eyes on the portraits seemed to watch her struggle.

The farther she advanced, the more her throat burned. Odd. Was she not moving past the fire? She bent, coughing away the discomfort, then stopped, horrified.

Smoke billowed out from a crack between floorboards and wall, from a door blending in against the dark wood. She shoved her shoulder against the paneling, and it gave. Air thick with smoke hovered near the ceiling inside of a small antechamber. Clara dropped to a crouch. Eye to eye with the legs of furniture, it appeared to be a sitting room, but no time to speculate whose. Flames crawled up the draperies on the far window, as did muffled shrieks behind a farther wall. Despite the heat, Clara's blood turned to ice. Someone was trapped, and she'd never be able to do this alone. Was there enough time to get help?

There'd have to be. Whirling, she ran back to the drawing room. The stench of burnt fabric and sweat violated last evening's scent of pine and fresh holly.

"More fire!" she hacked out as she bolted across the threshold. "It's worse, and someone is trapped."

Ben and Mr. Pocket, soot blackened and chests heaving, paused in whaling their draperies against what remained of the flames. Mr. Minnow stood to the side, clutching his portion of ripped brocade to his chest, hair askew but otherwise untouched by labor of any kind.

Mr. Pocket exchanged a glance with Ben, then they both sprinted toward her. Ben hollered over his shoulder at Mr. Minnow, "Finish the job, man!"

Gaining her side, Ben dipped his head. "Lead the way."

By the time she returned with the men in tow, smoke belched from the door like an angry dragon. Ben and the inspector charged into the room. Fear barreled into her heart—and squeezed. Was she to lose him again now that they were just starting to make amends?

Her hands curled into fists. Not if she could help it.

She tore back to the drawing room and raced over to Mr. Minnow, who stood exactly as they'd left him. The last rogue embers smoldered not five paces from him.

What a wastrel! She snatched the draperies out of his hands. "Mr. Minnow! Either put the rest of those flames out now or we shall all perish."

He gaped, arms flapping at his sides. "But how am I to do so?"

"Remove your nightshirt and bat them out." She huffed, then flew back to the real danger.

And real it was, more so from the smoke now than the flames. Inhaling the better air of the corridor, she charged into the room—just as glass shattered. Like a flock of demons, the black cloud poured out the window Ben had broken. Slowly, the room cleared, leaving behind the hacking and coughing of Ben and Mr. Pocket, her own labored breaths, and a dull thumping accompanied by a mewling cry.

Ben wheeled toward the sound. "There!"

The men dashed to the far wall, where a board had been nailed across a door. What on earth? What kind of villain barricaded helpless victims, then set fire to ensure their demise?

Grabbing a candlestick fallen to the floor, Ben wedged a corner of it behind the wood and pulled. The board crashed to the floor with a clatter. Mr. Pocket yanked on the knob, and Jilly flew out the door like a bat from an attic, screaming all the way. From the depths of the attached room, Mr. Tallgrass's curses swelled as black as the former smoke—but that was all. No real smoke or flames infected that room.

Ben dropped the candlestick. "Thank God."

"Indeed." Mr. Pocket rubbed a hand over his shorn head.

Clara shuddered, afraid to believe. Where might the next fire spring up? She picked her way past a tipped-over chair, edging to Ben's side. "Is it over? Truly?"

A muscle stood out on his neck like a steel rod, until he blew away the tension with a deep sigh. "Let us hope so." He cast her a sideways glance, and a shadow darkened his face. "You are trembling. Come, I'll see you to your room."

Offering his arm, he slipped his gaze to Mr. Pocket. "I believe you can handle Mr. Tallgrass, can you not, Inspector?"

Mr. Pocket leaned a hand against the doorframe and coughed, long and hard, then straightened as if he'd not just nearly hacked up a lung. "Righty-o. I've managed worse. See to the lady, Mr. Lane."

Wrapping her fingers around Ben's arm, she allowed him to lead her from the charred room and up to her chamber, grateful for his strength. The morning's peril and chaos had poked holes in her courage, draining her dry, so much so that she stumbled at the top of the stair.

Ben covered her hand with his strong fingers, steadying her. "Are you all right?"

The sleeve of his nightshirt molded against hard muscle, and for the first time, she realized she wore naught but a robe over her chemise, a thin one at that. No, she was definitely not all right.

"I am fine," she answered.

God, forgive me.

Willing her feet to behave, she managed to make it to the door of her chamber without further misstep. A miracle, really, for the heat of the man at her side—the one her body remembered despite what her mind might say—sped her heartbeat until it was hard to breathe.

She wanted to ask him to hold her. To wrap his arms around her as he had yesterday out in the woods and pretend nothing had changed between them. But when he pulled away and his sleeve rode up his arm, a black number marred his skin. She stared, wanting to turn away from the awful sight yet completely helpless to do so. The mark of a felon stared back at her. He was not the same man. How could he be?

The Ben she'd known—gentle and kind, compassionate almost to a fault—might never be the same again. Loss squeezed her chest, and a small cry escaped her lips.

Ben shoved down his sleeve and lifted her face to his. "Do I frighten you?"

She swallowed, throat burning as much from his question as from the remnants of acrid smoke. How was she to answer that? She feared the things he'd seen and had to do to survive, the sometime feral gleam in his eyes when he thought she wasn't looking. But him? Did she fear this man who was to have been her husband? Did not the same heart still beat inside his chest?

"No, I do not." She turned and fled into her chamber, closing the door between them. Leaning her back against the cool wood, she panted, fighting to catch her breath. It wasn't a lie, for in truth, she was even more afraid of the queer twinge deep inside her belly.

Hunger, yes, but for more than breakfast.

CHAPTER THIRTEEN

Ben strode to the door of the sitting room, tugging at his collar. Air. Just a draft of it. A moment on the front stoop to escape the left-over smoke permeating the manor. No one would miss him. At least no one had when he'd disappeared earlier to pen yet another batch of letters pleading for a fresh look into his case. Even should he gain his freedom by staying here the full twelve days, there was still the matter of recouping his estate funds from the Court of Chancery.

As he passed by, he smiled at Clara, who played cards with Miss Scurry. Near the hearth, Mr. Tallgrass pestered his brooding young attendant with instructions on properly roasting a chestnut. Mademoiselle Pretents looked out the window. Minnow hovered near Clara. And the inspector sorted through a box of ashes in hopes of finding a clue as to how the fire had started or a hint of who'd been wicked enough to intentionally trap Mr. Tallgrass and Jilly.

As Ben approached the threshold, a servant darted in, dropping a curtsy in front of him.

"Begging yer pardon, sir, but it's Boxing Day." The woman peeked up at him, then tucked her chin.

"And?" he asked.

She clutched and reclutched handfuls of her apron. Timid little thing, apparently. "There's a line o' tradesmen downstairs what are expecting their Christmas boxes, sir."

He ran a hand along his jaw. Why would she think it necessary to tell him such information? "Then I suppose you should give them their due, hmm?"

"That's just it, sir. There are none." She lifted her face, eyes shimmering. "I din't know what else to do, who else to go to."

So she came to him? He flattened his lips to avoid a glower, for surely such a look would push the woman into hysterics. "Has the butler not returned?"

"No, sir." She shook her head. "Mrs. Dram, the housekeeper, she's gone as well. Why, there's naught but a handful of us servants to manage, and most of those are still cleaning up from the fire."

Who invited guests without hiring proper staff? He grunted, for offering his true opinion would not be fit for mixed company. "Can you not simply send the tradesmen away?"

She wrung the life out of her apron. Were it a chicken, it would long since have died. "I tried, sir. I did." Her voice pitched to a whine. "They won't listen to the likes o' me. I fear I shall be overrun with the brutes."

The tone must've reached Clara's ears, for she rose and crossed the carpet, stopping alongside him. "What's wrong?" she whispered.

Mr. Minnow trailed her. "Is there a problem, Miss Chapman?"

Ben smothered a growl. Must the man track her like a dog on a scent? Ignoring Minnow, he spoke to Clara. "It seems some tradesmen are expecting their Christmas boxes, yet there are none to be given."

"Oh." Her brow crumpled. "That is dreadful."

"Miss Chapman." Miss Scurry, having been left alone at the card table, gathered her box and joined them. "Has the reckoning come?"

Clara smiled at her. "Don't fret, Miss Scurry. Just an issue of not having Christmas boxes for the tradesmen."

"Eh? What's that?" Mr. Tallgrass craned his neck their way. "Tradesmen expectin' boxes? Flappin' beggars!"

The little maid cringed and stepped behind Ben. Laughable, really, that she'd seek refuge behind a convict. If he rolled up his sleeve, revealing his brand, would she run away as Clara had?

Whirling from the window, Mademoiselle Pretents threw out her arms. "Shoo them away, *imbécile*. We are not their masters. We are the guests. They can have no claim against us."

Ben sighed. This was getting out of hand. "True, yet without the master in attendance, I suppose we are all the tradesmen have as his representative."

His proclamation lifted the inspector's head from his study of the ashes. A grey smudge smeared the tip of his big nose. "How do you know it's a *him*, Mr. Lane?"

"Mere speculation, Inspector. Nothing more." He slipped a glance at the little maid. "Go about your business, miss. I'll see to the tradesmen."

The woman darted out the door and down the hall.

Clara turned to him, admiration deepening the blue of her gaze. "How will you manage that?"

Indeed. How would he? But for the glimmer in Clara's eyes, the embers of respect, he must come up with something.

"Fie!" Mr. Tallgrass's voice rasped. "Grab some of the candlesticks and whatnot from around here, man, and shove it in a box. Give that to 'em. That's how I'd manage, and with a kick to their backsides to help 'em out the door besides."

"But these things are not ours to give." Clutching her box tighter, Miss Scurry whimpered, her mobcap flopping nearly to her eyes. "Oh! The reckoning of it all."

"Well." Clara bit her lip, a sure sign something brewed in that pretty head of hers. "I think I have an idea. I propose we each retrieve whatever trifles we can spare from our travel bags. An extra handkerchief. A hair comb. Perhaps a peppermint you've forgotten about and have tucked away in a pocket. I, for one, have brought along my sewing basket and may find an overlooked needle and thread to spare."

"Oh, lovely! Such a beautiful idea." The lines on Miss Scurry's face disappeared. "I may have just the thing." She shoved back her cap with her free hand as she disappeared out the door.

Ben watched her go. Hopefully she wasn't rushing off to wrap up her mice. Still, Clara's idea was worth a shot.

Mademoiselle Pretents flounced over to Clara, jabbing the air with a pointed finger. "My jewels have already been stolen, and now you want to take more? No! I will not have it."

The inspector set his box onto the side table nearest him, then rose. "Mademoiselle, unless you'd like me to rummage through your things, I suggest you find something to donate."

"Are you threatening me, Monsieur?"

He halted in front of her and folded his arms. "Without doubt."

"Gah! I have no more to say to you." Her face pinched, nearly squeezing her dark eyes closed. "Any of you!" She stormed out of the room like a winter squall.

The inspector chuckled. "That's the best thing she's ever said." Then he tipped his head at Clara. "A generous proposal on your part, miss. The world could use more like you."

Pink bloomed on Clara's cheeks, quite the contrast to Mademoiselle Pretents's angry red. Ben tried not to stare, but the temptation was beyond a mere mortal such as himself. Ahh, he'd missed that innocent flush.

"I couldn't agree more, Inspector," he murmured, the words sounding huskier than he had intended—which only deepened her pink to the blush of a June rose.

"Well, I think it's a bunch o' flap." Mr. Tallgrass shifted on his wheeled chair, listing to the side. "Oy me rumpus. Jilly!"

"I'll leave him to you this time." The inspector grumbled under his breath as he passed by Ben and fled the room.

Carping and cussing spewed out Tallgrass's mouth the entire time Jilly propped him upward. "First my bones are rattled, then I'm fed fare what 'tain't fit for a street sweeper, and next someone tries to burn me in my own chamber. Now this? No! I ain't gonna give no one nothing. Tradesmen be hanged, I say."

Mr. Minnow puffed out his chest and blocked Clara's view of the man. If nothing else, he was a protective fellow. Then again, so was a rodent over a piece of Stilton.

"I'm certain I may find some trivialities that will suffice, Miss Chapman. Shall I see you to your room to retrieve some of yours?" His arm shot out.

Clara tucked her hands behind her back and stepped closer to Ben. "Thank you, but no, Mr. Minnow. I am sure I can manage on my own."

Minnow deflated, cast a withering look at Ben, then slunk away like a tot who'd been told no for the first time.

Clara watched him go and took another step toward Ben. Not that he minded, but such daring while Tallgrass eyed them?

"I was hoping to have a word with you," she said.

He looked past her, over at Tallgrass, who'd blessedly gone back to berating Jilly and her chestnut roasting skills at the hearth. Still, one never knew when the man would lash out at them again. He guided Clara to the door with a nudge to the small of her back. "Out in the hall."

In the foyer, the lion head stared down at them. Ben smirked. Was this really any better?

Clara removed something from her pocket and held out her hand. A gold coin stared up at him.

He looked from the coin to her. "You're offering gold to a thief?"

She shoved her hand closer. "Go on. I should like your opinion of it."

Narrowing his eyes, he plucked the coin from her palm. Lightweight. Roughened edges. Perhaps over the centuries people had shaved bits off during times of dire need. One side was worn more than the other, a cross, or maybe an X, was at the center—impossible to read the letters ringing it. He flipped it over.

"Secundus casus." He tasted the words like a foreign fruit. At first he'd thought it an old Roman coin, but none ever read thus. "Interesting. Where did you get this?"

"Someone slipped it under my door yesterday. Can you tell me what it says?"

"Second chance," he drawled, but by the time the translation finished rolling off his tongue, he knew—and sucked in a sharp breath. "This was my charade last night, Clara."

"What does it mean?"

"I don't know." Behind him, the eyes of the lion burned into his back, and he stiffened. "The mysteries are starting to pile up in a great heap, are they not?"

"Sounds ominous." She tipped her face to his, searching his eyes for God knew what. "Should I be afraid?"

"No. As you told Miss Scurry, don't fret. Be watchful, yet don't worry. I would not willingly allow any harm to come to you." He reached for her hand and pressed her fingers around the coin, holding on longer than etiquette allowed. The warmth of her skin burned hotter than a summer day. How he'd missed this, a simple touch, hushed words shared by them alone. The way her blue gaze looked to him for strength. Desire stoked a fire in his gut.

He pulled away before he wrapped her in his arms and never let go. "Keep that coin. For whatever reason, someone wanted you to have it."

"But who? And why?"

"Sometimes all we have are questions." He shook his head. Lord knows he'd had his share of them while rotting in a gaol cell. "But there's really only one that matters."

She blinked, an endearing little wrinkle bunching her nose. "What's that?"

"Is God in control, or is He not?"

Chapter Fourteen

Second chance. Second chance. With each stab of Clara's needle through the fabric, she mulled over what the coin in her pocket could possibly mean. Though she'd had nearly an hour to herself in the sitting room to think on it, nothing came to mind.

Ben entered, breaking her concentration. He strolled across the carpet, hands behind his back. "How goes it? Am I the last one to donate to your worthy cause?"

"No, I'm still waiting for Miss Scurry and Mr. Minnow's contributions." After she nipped the thread with her teeth, she tucked away her needle and held up the finished project for Ben's inspection. "As for me, I've sewn six pouches from fabric scraps. Not brilliant, but serviceable. And far better than what the others have dropped off."

"And that would be. . . ?"

Gathering her sacks, large enough for a few coins or some pinches of snuff, she led Ben to a side table and set down her offering. Then she pointed at a twist of waxed paper. "Mr. Pocket dropped off a half-dozen comfits." She moved her finger onward to a string of cracked leather. "Mr. Tallgrass had Jilly deliver this old watch fob, though I doubt very much it will hold anything without breaking." Lastly, she swept her hand above a nearly empty glass vial. "And why on earth Mademoiselle Pretents thinks anyone would want a few specks of smelling salts is beyond me, but at least she gave something, so I didn't think it fair to chide her."

"Then hopefully my addition will be welcome." Ben's hands appeared from behind his back and he set down a pile of folded papers.

Fascinated at what he'd created, she retrieved one and held it to eye level. A miniature crane, creamy white, complete with long neck, wings, and an inked-in dot for an eye stared back at her. She looked from the crane to the man. "I didn't know you were a master at paper folding."

His gaze locked onto hers, one brow curving ever so slightly. "A man must have some secrets to keep a lady intrigued."

Warmth settled low in her tummy. La! She was more than intrigued with this man—and as confused about the sudden emotion he aroused in her as she was about the meaning of the coin in her pocket.

"Pardon me, miss, sir."

They both turned as the small maid entered and dipped a curtsy. "You asked, miss, and so I've counted. There are five tradesmen remaining downstairs. Two tired of waiting and have since left."

"Very good." Clara smiled at her. "We shall deliver the boxes shortly. Thank you, er. . . ?"

The short woman tucked her chin. "It's Betty, miss."

"Thank you, Betty."

Once again she curtsied, then darted out of the room—as the sound of laughter and conversation ambled in. Miss Scurry and Mr. Minnow crossed the threshold, the lady lifting her gaze to Mr. Minnow, a brilliant smile stealing years from her face. Mr. Minnow's elastic lips moved at a steady speed, engrossing the older lady with some sort of story. Regardless of the age difference, the two seemed to draw as much happiness in their companionship as a married couple might. Both carried an assortment of boxes.

Ben nudged Clara. "Looks like Minnow's found himself a lady friend. Feeling jealous?"

She ignored him, for any response would only fuel his teasing.

When Mr. Minnow paused for a breath, Clara cleared her throat, and the two new arrivals looked her way.

Immediately Mr. Minnow dashed over, bypassing her and Ben to set the boxes he'd been carrying on the table. Then with clipped steps, he stood at smart attention in front of Clara.

"I've brought you something." He clicked his heels twice, then pulled out a collection of small paper bags from his pocket. Balancing them in the crook of his arm, he held a single bag out to her. "This one is expressly for you."

"Why Mr. Minnow, very thoughtful of you."

Next to her, Ben did a poor job of concealing a disgusted sigh.

Once again she ignored him and reached for the offered gift, then unfolded the top of the bag. The scent of ginger wafted out. Inside were amber balls, the size of her pinkie fingertip. She smiled up at the fellow. "Ginger drops are a favorite of mine."

"Isn't that lovely!" Miss Scurry exclaimed.

Mr. Minnow grinned so widely, Clara feared his face might split. With a military pivot, he strode back to the table to add his donation to the rest.

Ben leaned close and whispered in her ear. "So that's why he always smells of Christmas cakes."

She tried to shoot him a scolding frown but failed, for in truth, he was right.

Miss Scurry turned from the table, where she'd set her boxes, as well—except for one she carried over to Clara. "I've brought something also, my dear. Would you like to see?"

The fine hairs at the back of Clara's neck lifted. Clearly the woman wanted her to take the box and open it. But if she did, would a mouse rise up and possibly escape? A shiver ran across her shoulders, feeling like a hundred little rodent feet.

Ben reached for the box. "May I?"

"Oh, yes! What an honor. What a delight." The old lady beamed at him.

Stepping aside from Clara, Ben removed the lid, then turned to her and tilted it so that she might see. Inside, nestled on a folded white kerchief, lay a penny.

Clara's eyes widened. "I hardly know what to say. This is more than generous, Miss Scurry."

"Tush! We can't send those fine tradesmen off with naught but trifles."

Mr. Minnow gained the lady's side and gathered her hand. "You are a true lady, madam." He bent and kissed her fingers.

Miss Scurry fluttered her free hand to her chest. "Oh! Such a gentleman."

Rolling his eyes at the two, Ben turned away from the dramatics and strode over to the table. "Let's get packing. Those men have waited long enough."

They joined him, and before all the boxes were opened, Clara said,

"We need only five for the tradesmen, but I thought it might be nice to make Betty one for all her hard work."

Between the four of them, it didn't take long to pack up the treasures. Clara even retrieved some red thread from her sewing basket and tied a bow on each one. "There."

"Beautiful!" Though only one word, Miss Scurry's voice warbled it like a song.

Ben stacked the boxes in his arms, and the pile sat precariously up to his neck.

Clara removed the top two. "You'll never make it down the stairs without dropping one. I'll go with you."

Miss Scurry clapped her hands. "Lovely! Now, Mr. Minnow, about that story you were telling me. . ."

"Ahh, yes! A real thriller, is it not?" He fairly skipped over to the settee and patted the cushion beside him. "Should you like to hear the end?"

"Indeed, sir."

Clara exchanged a glance with Ben as they exited the room.

Out in the foyer, well out of earshot, Ben smiled down at her. "Quite a little friendship those two have struck up."

"I think it's good for both of them."

"And what do you think is good for us?"

"I. . ." Her mouth dried. How to answer that?

He winked. "No answer required."

Heat flooded her cheeks. Thankfully, he averted his all-knowing gaze and turned down a rather poorly lit corridor. She followed at his side, uncertain what else to say. So she said nothing—and neither did he, until they came to a plain stairway near the back of the house.

Ben paused on the first stair. "This seems the most logical route."

She followed. The lower they descended, the stronger the aroma of cabbage soup. Clara's stomach clenched—as did her heart—but not from the scent. Cabbage soup had been a favorite of her father's. A dish he cherished even more than he did her. During his last days, she'd tried to make it just to please him, refining the amount of salt, the addition of ham bits, the sprinkling of a fine grating of pepper. Nothing satisfied him, least of all her. Just one more example of her failing to gain his love before he died. Her step faltered, and the boxes jiggled.

Ben reached the landing and turned to her. "Are you all right?"

Shoving down the sour memory, she forced a smile. "Yes, just a slip."

She cleared the last three stairs without incident while he waited. Then they navigated the barren maze of the downstairs world side by side. Finally, they found the kitchen.

Inside, five men rose from the slab of a table at center. Each wore work-stained clothing and frowns. A few of them exchanged glances. Without a word, all lined up with their hands out.

Ben went to the far end while Clara handed one of her boxes to the first man.

"Thank you for your service," she said.

He nodded his head and gruffed out, "Thank ye."

Stepping to the next man, she held out his gift. "Thank you for your service."

But he didn't take it. He just stared, his eyes sharp and black as basalt. He studied her with a curl to his upper lip, like a mongrel facing an unknown adversary. He smelled of dogs as well. "Wouldn't stay 'ere if I were you. A house without its master is like a body without its soul."

He snatched the box from her.

She recoiled a step, wobbling for a moment. Must everything about this place cause her to teeter? She sucked in a breath. Nine more days. Just nine.

But what would tomorrow bring?

The Fourth Day

DECEMBER 27, 1850

CHAPTER FIFTEEN

Clara rushed through her morning routine, shivering all the while. Not that she could blame the housemaid for having an unlit hearth when she awoke. Hopefully more servants would arrive today from the nearby village now that the staff's one-day-a-year holiday was over.

She rose and smoothed her skirts, then crossed to the door. On second thought, she returned to the dressing table and picked up the gold coin, secreting it in her pocket. Ben was right. Someone wanted her to have it—no sense finding the coin stolen when she returned. Mademoiselle Pretents had yet to find her missing jewels, despite her snooping about the great house and Mr. Pocket's detective skills.

Reaching for the knob, Clara swung the door open, then stopped. The hall was empty, save for a pair of ice skates blocking her exit from her chamber. She picked them up with a smirk. Too big to fit under her door, eh?

She hurried downstairs to the dining room, hoping she wasn't the only one to receive such a gift. Once she cleared the landing and wove her way from foyer to corridor, her hope turned into reality. Mr. Minnow strolled ahead of her, a pair of skates slung over one of his thin shoulders.

He turned, and a huge smile split his face. "Ahh, Miss Chapman. A hearty good morning to you, and so it shall be, for I see you carry a pair of skates yourself."

She gripped her skates with both hands before the man could offer his arm yet again. "Indeed I do, sir. Do you suppose our elusive host is responsible?"

"I would imagine so, my pet."

The intimate name rankled. She'd hoped he'd tire of using it by now. Clearly not. "Mr. Minnow," she began, "I would prefer it if you would not call me—"

"La!" Mademoiselle Pretents blustered up from behind. "I am given ice skates but not my jewels. What's this? You have them, too?"

The three of them entered the dining room before Clara could answer, but truly, did the woman really need confirmation when she could see they each toted a pair?

Ahead, Miss Scurry turned in her chair, where she took breakfast at the head of the table. Her elfish chin twitched when she smiled. "So lovely!" Then she swiveled back to Ben and Mr. Pocket, seated on either side of her. "You were right, gentlemen. We have all been blessed with ice skates."

In the nearest corner, three other pairs leaned against the wall. Clara laid hers next to them, then headed for the sideboard.

Ben and Mr. Pocket rose from their seats, waiting until she and Mademoiselle Pretents filled their bowls with a thin, gruel-like substance and came to the table. Ben held out the chair next to him, and Clara rewarded him with a smile.

"Thank you," she said.

He leaned toward her. "You may not be too thankful when you taste that porridge."

After one bite, she shoved the bowl away. Even a swine would turn up his nose at this slop.

Ben reached for the teapot and filled her cup, adding an extra sugar drop and more milk than usual. He winked. "For your skating stamina."

As usual, he was right, for the tea filled her tummy and warmed her to her fingers and toes.

Mr. Pocket stood and addressed the table. "In honor of our absent host, I propose we accept the challenge and resign ourselves to the frozen pond out back."

"Pah!" Mademoiselle Pretents spat out. "Go ahead and run off, Inspector. You are worthless at finding my jewels, anyway. But I do not skate. Nor do I see *Monsieur Tallgrass* having to submit himself to the cold."

Mr. Pocket pursed his lips, sticking them out nearly as far as his nose. "Speaking of which, has anyone seen him this morning?"

Mumbles circled the table.

"Right. Well, I'll go check on the fellow, then meet up with you, eh?" He exited before anyone could refuse.

Everyone grabbed their skates, except for Mr. Minnow, who not only finished off his porridge but was currently scraping out the dregs of hers as well. After retrieving their coats, they gathered in the foyer. Then the group roamed a few hallways with Ben in the lead, until discovering a door at the back.

They all paused, waiting for Mr. Pocket to join them. They waited so long, warmth trickled between Clara's shoulder blades. "Perhaps we could begin without Mr. Pocket?"

Ben nodded. "He seems a capable-enough fellow to find his way to the pond."

Clara turned to Miss Scurry. "Are you sure you'll be able to manage this?"

"Such a dear!" the woman twittered. She set down her box of mice and tucked it aside in a corner, then peered up at Clara, a sparkle in her eye belying the wrinkles on her face. "But you see, I am quite capable."

The woman darted outside.

"I suspect there is more than meets the eye in that one," said Ben.

Clara exchanged a glance with him, then exited as he held the door for her. Outside, a draft of wind nipped her cheeks, but oh how lovely to be away from the manor's dark-paneled walls. A path had been shoveled, bare grass peeking up and crunching beneath her shoes as she walked. Thicker blankets of snow snuggled among tree roots and crested in piles against the north side of rocks. The sun shone with glorious brilliance, and when the next gust blew, glittering faery dust sprinkled over their hats and coats. The group stopped at the pond's edge, a great swath of which had been cleared of snow.

Ben guided Clara to a downed log, likely set there for just such a purpose. "Shall I help you?" he asked.

"Do you really think you need to?" She gave him a knowing smile.

He returned it—then added a wink and crouched in front of her. The touch of his hand guiding her foot into the skate sent a charge up her leg. A shameful response, but completely delicious. His head bowed over his work, a small blessing, that. For if he glanced up now, she'd be undone.

He buckled on her skates in silence, but she had no doubt as to what memories played in his mind. Two winters ago at just such a skating party, he'd first pledged his love. Despite the cold, she loosened her scarf. Keeping warm was not going to be an issue, for heat burned a trail from tummy to heart.

Standing, Ben offered his hand. "Off you go."

Refusing to meet his gaze, she righted herself and sailed onto the ice. Miss Scurry already whirled and twirled near the edge, while Mr. Minnow yet struggled to shove his long feet into his skates. Mademoiselle Pretents didn't even try to accommodate. Skates forgotten on the ground at her feet, she stood with her back to them, arms folded, a dark grey smear on the lovely day. Why had she even bothered to join them?

Turning from the sight, Clara dug in her blades. Brisk air tingled on her face, driving her onward, faster and—a big hand reached for hers and spun her around.

Ben laughed, his voice low. "Think you can outskate me, madam?" His eyes sharpened with a glimmer of victory.

Her breath caught in her throat. This close, his words puffed out on little clouds of vapor, warming the skin of her forehead. La! Every part of her was warm, for if he tugged with just a bit more pressure, he'd pull her into his arms. She tried to force a scowl, a nearly impossible feat when all she really wanted to do was surrender to the grin that begged release. "I should've known you'd accost me on the ice, sir."

"Yes." He leaned closer, his brow nearly touching hers. "You should have."

He grabbed her other hand and they set off, gliding in rhythm, moving together, blades cutting a fresh pattern into the ice. Closing her eyes, she pretended they were younger, before sorrow had stolen their innocence. She could live here, in this moment, content with the strength of his gait and the way his fingers gripped hers, so firm yet gentle.

Thank You, God, she prayed, silent of voice yet loud of spirit. This was a holy time, this sacred oneness—and her heart broke afresh, for indeed they should have been one by now. Even so, she soaked in this reality, memorizing his strength and grace and—

Without warning, a loud cry defiled the moment.

Chapter Sixteen

"Wait here!" Ben shoved off, leaving Clara safely behind—hopefully. Too much weight on the ice where Minnow had broken through could send them both into a frigid bath. On the far side of the pond, each time Minnow surfaced, he howled another cry for help.

Digging in his blades, Ben tucked his head and sped toward the fellow. Ten or so paces from the man, he scraped to a stop. With one hand, he unwound the long scarf from his neck, then dropped to a crawl, displacing his weight. Testing the ice with each advance, he edged forward, trying desperately to detect any cracking sounds above the racket of Mr. Minnow's splashing and thrashing.

"Grab the side of the ice where you first went in," Ben shouted.

Minnow flailed, too panicked to do anything but froth up muddy pond water.

Judging the distance, Ben halted and knotted one end of the scarf. He secured the other end to his hand and threw it. "Grab on!"

Two tries later, the man snagged the fabric. Ben crawled backward, tugging the wriggling fellow out of the hole like a fish. Minnow shrieked all the way, but Ben didn't stop until they were halfway to shore. Deeming it safe enough to stand, he rose and let go of the scarf, then raced to Minnow, who still lay flat on the ice. When he reached him, Ben sucked in a breath.

The man's left leg jutted sideways between kneecap and ankle, a place where no leg ought to bend. No wonder he'd bawled.

"Clara!" Ben called, and she sailed to his side. "Help me get Mr. Minnow up."

He grabbed one shoulder, the side with the broken leg, and Clara took the other. Together they hauled the man to solid ground, his drenched, muddy clothing soaking into each of their sides.

"Set him down," Ben instructed.

Removing their skates to Minnow's cries and repeated interjections of "Oh my!" from Miss Scurry was harrowing enough, but Mademoiselle Pretents's running commentary as they did so pushed Ben over the edge.

He stood and towered over the grey demon. "Mademoiselle, call this man *stupidé* or an *imbécile* one more time, and I shall retrieve my scarf to stop up your mouth."

Her lips pinched shut, rippling like a clamshell, and she stalked to the manor. Her billowing skirts created a wider path to tow Minnow. Miss Scurry fluttered behind them all.

The path to the big house ran at a slight incline. Ben leaned forward to compensate, hopefully taking the bulk of the burden from Clara. Once inside, he paused, glancing past the moaning Minnow to Clara. "You holding up?"

She nodded. "Better than he, poor man."

"Let's press on, then."

A few grunts and many cries later, they managed to drape the fellow on the largest settee in the sitting room.

Chest heaving from the exertion, Clara leaned against the sofa's back and lifted her eyes to him. "Now what? Call for a physician or send him to one?"

Miss Scurry twittered in the doorway, once again clutching her box to her chest. "Yes, indeed! What do we do, Mr. Lane? Oh, the reckoning. I feared it for him, I did."

"No!" Minnow howled. "I cannot leave. I'll lose my prize. Please, Mr. Lane."

Ben kneaded a muscle at the back of his neck, unsure if he ought feel pleased or cursed that they all looked to him for answers. Scrubbing his jaw, he crossed to the hearth, stalling for time and debating what to do. He snagged the scuttle and hefted what coal remained onto the grate. One thing he knew for sure—it wouldn't do for any of them to take a chill.

The next yelp from Minnow made up his mind, and he wheeled about. "Prize or not, it's cruel to allow Mr. Minnow to suffer. I shall go for a carriage at once, and we'll send a servant along with him to the nearest physician."

Minnow started weeping.

Clara knelt at his side, taking one of his hands in hers. "Mr. Minnow, please. Do try to bear up."

"Oh, the pain," he wailed. "And the loss!"

"I understand, sir, but. . ." She paused, as did Minnow, who sucked in a shaky breath and held it as if his very life hinged on her next words.

"Your wish was for a companion, was it not?" Clara asked.

Ben stepped closer, intrigued by the tilt of her head. She was up to something, for she used such a pose whenever trying to persuade him.

Minnow nodded.

"I think, sir, that you have received it already." Clara glanced at the doorway. "Wouldn't you agree, Miss Scurry?"

The older woman pattered in, cheeks flushed from their outside excursion. "How's that, dear?"

"Are you not now one of Mr. Minnow's friends?"

"Why, yes! I suppose that I am. How lovely." The woman drew near, quickly at first, then with more tentative steps. Finally, she stopped and lifted the lid on her box. Eight white mice rose on hind legs, scratching the sides to get out.

"Ch-ch-ch," she clucked and poked one to knock it back, then she beamed down at Minnow. "My friends are yours as well. Would you like to meet them? Ahh, but I thought you would." Her finger rested like a benediction upon each mouse as she spoke. "Here is Love and Joy, Rest, Want, and Peril." Hesitating, she shook her head, and her face darkened as she nudged the final three in the rump. "And here is Distress, Disease, and Turnip."

Ben studied the woman. Had she lost her senses?

But then as suddenly, her eyes cleared and the dimples at the corners of her mouth reappeared. "I am delighted to share my companions with you, Mr. Minnow, being that you are now one of my dearest friends. My, but we shall have a time of it, will we not? Until the day of reckoning, of course." She pressed the lid back on top of her box and clutched it to her chest. "But now my dears are weary, and so we shall retire." Without another word, she whirled and scurried off.

"And there you have it, sir. Your time at Bleakly Manor has been profitable, indeed." Clara pulled her hand from Minnow's. "Shall we send you to get mended up, then?"

Minnow's lower lip quivered. "I. . .I had hoped that companion would've been you, my pet."

Even in pain the man didn't give up. Serious rival or not, Ben stepped closer to Clara. "A friend is a friend no matter the age or size."

"Indeed," Minnow conceded, until a shudder ran the length of his body and he groaned, his face draining of colour.

Ben snapped into action, calling out as he strode to the door. "Clara, would you retrieve a blanket to cover Mr. Minnow while I arrange things?"

"Of course." Her sweet voice faded as he entered the hall.

Mr. Pocket careened around a corner, nearly bumping into Ben. The inspector, dressed for the outdoors, jumped back a step. "What's this? I was just coming to join you outside and here you are, looking as if you've rolled in snow and dipped half your body in mucky water. What's afoot now, Mr. Lane?"

Ben hesitated, the same eerie feeling of being watched shivering across his shoulders. No, more likely he was simply chilled to the marrow. He shook off the strange sensation. "Mr. Minnow took an unfortunate spill into the pond, breaking his leg in the process. We need a carriage brought 'round for transport to the nearest doctor."

"I shall see to it." The inspector pivoted and dashed down the corridor before Ben could say anything.

Running his fingers through his hair, Ben set off toward the stairway leading down to the servants' quarters. All the while, he mulled over the odd behavior of the inspector. Ben hadn't been asking or commanding the man to retrieve a carriage. Why such instant accommodation?

A gruff-looking maid, the antithesis of Betty, exited the stairwell before he could descend. She neither met his gaze nor acknowledged his presence.

He blocked her from hurrying past him. "Excuse me, but we need an attendant to travel with one of the guests to the nearest physician. Could you see about finding one?"

She whirled and marched back down the stairs.

He watched her go, unsure if the woman was mute or just rude. A stranger household could not be found in all of England. Hopefully she'd carry out his instructions. Time would tell, no doubt.

And time he ought to retrieve his scarf. Retracing his steps to the back door, he pulled it open and stalked down to the pond. Once on the ice, he half slid and half walked to where his scarf lay in a heap. He picked it up, then wheeled about and dissected the path that Minnow had skated.

Off to one side, part of the man's skate lay forgotten. Could the silly fellow not even buckle on his skates properly? Bending, he scooped it up and squinted at the broken bit. File marks scratched the metal at the edges where the blade had snapped. He peered closer. Someone weakened that metal, in hopes that after not too many glides, the skate would break and Minnow would take a vicious tumble, especially if he were going fast.

Moving on, he scrutinized the pond near where Minnow had cracked through the ice. The area had been shoveled, just like the rest

Or had it?

Dropping to one knee, he brushed the ice with his fingertips. Ridges marred the surface. So, this hadn't been merely shoveled. It had been shaved, thinned, so that a jab with a broken skate would snap it like a broken bone. He rose slowly, then turned and strode back to the manor. Minnow had been targeted. But why?

And by whom?

The Fifth Day

DECEMBER 28, 1850

Chapter Seventeen

Oh, for the blazing sun of an August day. La! Truth be told, Clara would settle for the weak warmth of an April afternoon. Lifting her skirts in one hand and gripping her sewing basket in the other, she dashed down the staircase faster than decorum dictated, in hopes of creating some kind of heat. Since she'd arrived five nights ago, the manor had grown chillier with each passing day.

Hopefully the turn of weather was not making Aunt Mitchell's cough any worse. With effort, she shoved that thought aside. Of course she'd receive word should her aunt's health take a dangerous turn. Wouldn't she?

Upping her pace, she hurried to the sitting room. As she neared the door, Mr. Pocket's voice heated the air inside.

"Stuff and poppycock, I say."

Clara tiptoed to the doorway.

"Pah!" Mademoiselle Pretense swooped over to the man like a falcon on the kill.

Mr. Pocket kept his big nose in his book, refusing to look up.

"I tell you it is a bad omen. Dimwit!" The French tempest stamped her foot. "Everyone knows if a Yule log burns out before Twelfth Night, a year of bad luck follows."

Clara bit her lip, unsure if she ought to enter such a fray.

Spying her from across the room, Ben gave her a wink. A familiar gesture, yet her heart never failed to skip a beat, even if she hadn't figured out where their relationship yet stood.

"Mademoiselle." Ben tapped the fire poker against the hearth bricks, and Clara couldn't help but wonder if he had the urge to use it on Mademoiselle Pretents. "There was no possible way Miss Chapman and I could have hauled back a log large enough to last the entire holiday. Today is well spent, but I assure you, I shall retrieve more wood on the morrow. So you see, it is not a matter of bad luck whatsoever, but merely poor planning on the part of our host."

"What a bunch of flap. Jilly! Turn me around." The girl wheeled Mr. Tallgrass about from where he peered out the window. Facing them, he sneered. "The lot of us ain't had nothing but black luck since we arrived. Were Minnow here, he'd agree. But oh. . .he's nursing a broken leg now, ain't he?" Gruff laughter shook his bones, and he canted to one side. "Oy me rumpus. Jilly!"

The girl sprang into action, and Clara took the opportunity to scoot to Ben's side, clutching her basket handle with both hands. "Sounds like the natives are getting restless."

"Worse. They've taken to blowing poison darts at one another." He smiled down at her, then angled his head toward a leather-bound book on the mantel, a single red ribbon peeking out from the pages. "Thankfully, I discovered a library in the east wing and have taken refuge in the pages of a book, escaping any direct hits myself."

Across the room, Miss Scurry sat alone on a chair, bent over her box and trembling so that the fabric of her skirt shook. Clearly, she had not been so fortunate as Ben.

The sight broke Clara's heart, for it struck too close to home. Was Aunt even now suffering shakes and tremors all alone? Swallowing down the image, Clara lifted up a prayer for Aunt Deborha and strode over to Miss Scurry. "Are you well, ma'am?"

"It is wrong," she murmured without looking up. "Entirely wrong. But then, perhaps, the world was never meant to go right."

Had the woman even heard her? She tried again. "Miss Scurry?"

Slowly, the older lady lifted a blank face. Her eyes narrowed, little creases etching lines into her skin. How many years had this woman seen? How much tribulation?

Then just as suddenly, a smile flashed. "Such a dear, you are. Do you suppose Mr. Minnow has received his reckoning?"

"I am sure he is on the mend and feeling much better already. Furthermore, I have no doubt you will be able to visit him by the time we are finished here."

"Oh, but his parting foreshadows the final one, I fear. Something is about to happen. Ch-ch-ch." She wrapped her hands tighter around her box, the lace of her collar quivering, the black ribbon of her quizzing glass quaking as well.

What kind of grim prediction was that? Did the woman have gypsy blood running in her veins to foretell such an awful fortune? Clara opened her mouth to respond, but the old lady once again bowed her head over her precious mice, ending the conversation by murmuring endearments to her furry companions.

Clara returned to the hearth, where Ben poked at the few remaining coals. He slipped her a glance, which despite the lack of flames, shot warmth through her heart.

She spoke in a low tone, unwilling for vulture-like ears to hear and peck her words to death. "I fear Miss Scurry is overwhelmed with what's been happening. If only—"

A deep thudding on the front door interrupted, and she jumped, skittish as the filly she'd once owned. She glanced toward the door, as did everyone else.

"Be at peace, Clara." Ben rose and squeezed her shoulder. "A servant will see to it."

More bangs followed.

And again.

"You sure about that, Lane?" Mr. Pocket set down his book and rose from the settee, then strode to the door.

The way they were slowly dwindling in number, was it safe for the man to go off on his own? She peered up at Ben. "Perhaps you ought to go with him."

"The inspector is a capable man." He released his hold of her. "But if you wish it."

With the exit of the only two able-bodied men, tension pulled the silence of the room into an almost unbearable tautness. Whom would Mr. Pocket and Ben usher in once the front door was opened?

Quietly, a low chant crept in from the foyer, slowly gaining in strength. Beautiful voices grew louder, raised in song.

"Fie!" A curse ripped past Mr. Tallgrass's lips. "What rubbish."

A lovely rendition of "Coventry Carol" held Clara in place like a sweet embrace, drawing her and the others toward it—save for Mr. Tallgrass. Jilly left him behind, following as far as the sitting-room door.

Clara crossed to Ben, huddling close for whatever warmth he

might share. The open door allowed in not only the chorus of five carolers, but a wicked icy draft as well. Cold air coiled beneath her skirt hem and skimmed up her legs. Fighting a shiver—for surely Ben would force her to return to the sitting room if he suspected she were chilled—she focused instead on the chorus.

Harmony heightened and dipped in perfect rhythm as the five singers crooned, all bright eyed and merry despite the minor key of their tune. The women, two of them, wore matching cloaks of deep green, and the men contrasted in caramel-coloured overcoats. Smart bonnets and top hats tipped back as they lifted their faces for a crescendo.

Clara's spirit couldn't help but be lifted along with the swell. Giving in to the magic of the moment, she thanked God for small gifts such as this. Mademoiselle Pretents and Mr. Tallgrass were entirely wrong. Silly naysayers. With music so melodious, ill luck didn't stand a chance this day.

But then a tremble crept down her spine as she remembered exactly what day it was and why the carolers had chosen this song above all others. December 28. Childermas. The day commemorating the massacre of innocents in the attempt to kill the infant Jesus.

The lovely spell shattered into shards of despair.

"You all right?" Ben whispered into her ear.

"I..." How to answer? That all she could imagine now were broken little bodies of wee babes and tots? Bloodied and ruined. Her stomach turned. *Pull yourself together, Clara.*

She peered up at Ben, hoping her skewed thoughts didn't show on her face. "I believe I shall go get my shawl."

He gazed at her, his stare dissecting truth from bone, yet he said nothing, just gave her a nod.

Whirling, the haunting music pushed her onward—until the horrid gaze of the lion she must pass under slowed her steps. Throbbing started in her temples, and her blood drained to her feet. Surely the thing didn't see her, didn't mark her as prey to be devoured. So why did she suddenly feel like one of those innocent babes in the carol?

The Sixth Day

DECEMBER 29, 1850

CHAPTER EIGHTEEN

The wagon bumped over the same route to the woods Ben had taken four days earlier with Clara. This time, however, he wouldn't offer his coat to his companion, even though the inspector's big nose was reddened by the wind. With a "Walk on!" and a snap of the reins, Ben urged the horses forward. The best he would do for Mr. Pocket was get them to the break of the trees more quickly.

Hunching into his coat, the inspector pulled down his hat brim. "I've noticed you and Miss Chapman are well acquainted."

The next gust of wind hit him as sideways as the question, and he turned his face from it. Not an indictment from the man, just an innocent observation—laced with innuendo. But why? Of all the topics the inspector could've brought up, he'd chosen Clara?

Ben shifted on the seat. "You could say that."

"I believe I just did." Pocket sniffed, his nose growing redder by the minute. "She's been promised quite a sum if she remains the duration. Is her situation dire without those funds?"

Ben measured his words and his tone. No sense offering the man more than should be his. "Perhaps you should ask the lady yourself."

"I would, if I could ever get a word with her alone. You always seem to be nearby. Which makes me wonder..." Pocket turned to him, his head peeking out from his greatcoat like a turtle from its shell. "What do you stand to gain?"

A direct question, but still a covert attack—one that he wasn't quite sure how to parry. "Sorry?" he asked.

"Were you to marry the lady, why then, whatever is hers rightfully becomes yours. Don't tell me the thought hasn't crossed your mind."

Marry? The word bounced as pell-mell through his skull as the wheels juddering on the frozen ground. It had been simple once, straightforward, but now all the *ifs* of marriage tangled into a big snarl. *If* all his correspondence was answered, *if* he regained his freedom as promised, and *if* his family estate was restored, would Clara still have him? A branded convict?

He snapped the reins again, driving the horses much too fast toward the wood's edge. Pocket's head jerked up and down from the pace, and Ben set his jaw, staring straight ahead, refusing to make eye contact with the inspector. The rage burning up his neck and spreading like wildfire over his face would clearly be seen. Whoever had done this to him and Clara would pay dearly.

Shaving minutes off his last trek to the woods, he yanked the horses to a stop and set the brake. He hopped down and turned into the wind, brisk air stinging his skin. He drank it in like sweet, sweet nectar.

Rummaging at the back of the wagon, Pocket retrieved two axes, then walked to Ben's side and handed one over. "Here you go, Lane."

He grabbed the handle by the throat and hefted the blade over his shoulder, smirking at the irony. Only a week ago he'd have given anything for an ax or sledgehammer to break out of Millbank, with a few extra blows rained down upon the heads of his captors along the way. And now? Here he was, tromping into the woods with a sharp blade in his hands and a lawman at his side. Despite what anyone said, God surely did have a sense of humour.

Scanning the area for any dead trees, he wondered aloud, "Any luck figuring out who stole the jewels or started the fire, Inspector?"

Pocket shook his head. "Nothing solid, but I have my suspicions."

Ben glanced at him sideways. "Such as?"

Pocket snuffled, a great drop of moisture having gathered on the end of his nose. "I never accuse without solid evidence."

"Would that all law keepers shared your convictions."

Pocket's brows disappeared beneath his hat brim.

"Come now, sir." Ben smirked. "No need to continue the charade. I know you're here to keep an eye on me. I just haven't figured out why."

The inspector grunted, neither confirming nor denying the accusation.

Their trek continued in silence. Pausing at the crest of a ravine, Ben pointed down the slope at a snapped-off tree, the top half of the trunk lying downward, with the splintered ends still attached. A wind must have knocked it over last season.

"Looks like you've found our next Yule log," said the inspector.

The footing was tricky, but they set about taking turns swinging at the part of the trunk still clinging to the base. Once that was freed, and any frozen bits broken loose where the rest of it lay in the snow, they could haul it back to the wagon.

"The way I see it, Inspector," Ben said between swipes, "Tallgrass isn't physically able to steal, and Miss Scurry hasn't the mental capacity. That leaves you."

Pocket's ax stopped.

Chest heaving, Ben paused his next swing, as well. "Or the more obvious Mademoiselle Pretents."

"Interesting observation." Arching his back, Pocket removed his hat and swiped his brow. Then he straightened and faced Ben. "Yet you've conveniently left off naming yourself or Miss Chapman."

A slow smile curved his mouth. "Do you really think I'd incriminate her or myself?"

"Touché, Mr. Lane." Pocket inhaled so deeply, his chest puffed out. "I've got the rest of this part, I think. Why don't you go down to the end and pry the wood from the frozen ground?"

Wheeling about, Ben took his smile with him, convinced the inspector truly had no knowledge yet of the mischief maker's identification. The man's pride simply would not allow him to admit it.

Leaning his weight into his heels, Ben slid-walked deeper into the ravine. Maybe it would be better to assess the trunk midway before reaching the bottom. He turned partway—and a loud crack exploded.

He flew sideways. Snow, sticks, rocks mashed into his face as he hit the ground. Flailing, he tumbled headlong into the gorge, then slammed to a stop. He lay, breathing hard. Maybe. Hard to tell. Sound receded. Only a buzzing noise remained, irritating and high-pitched. Heat leaked down his cheek, from temple to chin. Each beat of his heart pumping out more thick warmth from his body to the cold ground.

But at least the thing was still beating.

"Lane?"

His name was far off. Like he'd heard in a nightmare once. No, at Millbank, from the guard outside his door, catcalling through the metal. Was he back there again? Had he never left? He clawed the ground, and his skull seemed to bust in half.

"You all right, Lane?" The words were closer now. Heavy breaths attached to them.

He groaned and pressed the heel of his hand to his head. Sticky fluid suctioned the two together.

A strong arm hauled him to his feet, and he stood on shaky legs, watching the world spin in a white haze. When he pulled his hand from his head, it came away bloody.

"What. . ." He staggered. "What happened?"

"My blade flew off, grazing you. Lucky you turned when you did, or you'd have taken the full brunt of it at the back of your skull." Pocket held up his ax shaft, pointing to the end of it where the sharp hunk of iron should've been. "Someone tampered with my ax."

Chapter Nineteen

Pulling the last stitch through a stocking scarred by previous mending, Clara used the slack to tie a knot, then nipped the thread with her teeth. The chill in the sitting-room air nipped her right back. She tucked the stocking into her basket of sewing, trying hard to pretend she was sitting in Aunt's home instead of a cold manor.

Adjacent to her, Mademoiselle Pretents huddled on a chair, hands clutching a cup of tea near her face, seeking what warmth might be found. "What is taking so long, eh? I'll tell you. Those stupid men are probably lost in the woods. La! But all this cold is not good for my complexion."

Near the empty hearth, Mr. Tallgrass sneered. "Listen to you carping about yer skin. Such a little dainty, are we? A precious, tiny flower? Well, I'm freezing me rumpus off!"

Mademoiselle Pretents glared at him over the rim of her cup. "Unfortunately, your lips are still attached and working."

"So are yours, you shrewish bag o'—"

"Mr. Tallgrass!" Clara cut him off before he fired any more volleys. "I am sure Mr. Lane and Mr. Pocket will return shortly with a new Yule log. Let us wait in peace."

"He does not know the meaning of the word." Mademoiselle Pretents slammed down her cup, rattling the saucer beneath. "He barely grasps *ze* English language."

Clara clenched her teeth. This was going to be a very long day.

A rustle of skirts flurried into the room. Miss Scurry entered, scampering as quickly as one of her mice. "Such devastation. Such loss." The old lady's voice tightened into a shrill cry. "I have lost Love!"

"Oh flap." Dragging the back of his hand across his mouth, Mr. Tallgrass wiped off a fleck of spittle, then flicked it onto the floor. "I should think at yer age love would be the last thing on yer mind, you crazy old titmouse."

"But Love is gone!" Turning to Clara, Miss Scurry held out her box. "Do say you shall help. She's only just gone missing. She can't have gotten far."

A prickle ran across the nape of Clara's neck. The woman wanted her to look for a mouse? She'd spent her twenty-five years avoiding the things. And if she did find the rodent, she'd surely scare it away with a scream.

"Miss Scurry." She spoke slowly, praying for wisdom. How to dissuade the woman from searching, yet comfort her obvious grief? "I am sorry for your loss, but your mouse could be anywhere in such a great manor."

The lady shook her head, her ruffled cap flopping to one side. "Not anywhere, exactly. I had my pets upstairs. Do say you'll come along."

"Oui, go." Mademoiselle Pretents shooed them off with a sweep of her hand before she collected her teacup. "And good riddance."

Some choice. Remain in a room of vipers or search for a rodent. Sighing, Clara tucked her sewing basket against the side of the settee and stood. Miss Scurry led her to the grand staircase, but curiously enough, the old woman didn't stop on the first floor, where their chambers were located. She continued on, exiting on the second-floor landing—where the men resided.

Clara stayed the woman with a touch to her sleeve. "Why were you up here?"

"The reckoning, of course." Miss Scurry blinked up at her, as if she'd just explained the workings of the universe in layman's terms.

Clara's brow pinched. Though she tried, no sense could be made of the woman's strange words. "I'm afraid you'll have to give me more information than that if I am to help you."

Miss Scurry held up her box, and Clara prayed all the while that the kerchief crammed into the hole on the side would not slip loose.

"My pets must romp, Miss Chapman. No good being shut in a box all the time." She whirled and scampered to the opening of a long corridor, the mirror image of the one that held the women's chambers one flight below. "With the men out collecting wood, I thought to let my companions run the length of this carpet and back. No one to step on them, you see."

It made sense, somewhat. Clara studied the hall. Two doors, one closer and one farther. Same paneled wood. Same carpet runner. But clearly no white mouse scuttled about. She turned to the old lady. "What happened?"

"Oh, such a frolic!" Miss Scurry's whole face lit. "Many happy paws, racing about. All came when I called, except for Love. I fear she darted beneath one of the doors."

Advancing, Clara stopped in front of the first door and squatted. There was a small gap, much like the one beneath hers. Perhaps a mouse had dashed inside, but clearly neither she nor Miss Scurry had any right to enter. She straightened and faced the woman. "These chambers are not ours. Let us wait until Mr. Lane and Mr. Pocket return. Surely they will help us."

Tears sprouted at the corners of the old woman's eyes. The first rolled down her parchment cheeks, then more, until wet trails dripped from her chin. Her lips quivered, and her face folded into grief. "Oh," she wailed. "I fear it will be too late for Love by then."

The old lady's sorrow hit Clara hard in the heart, and her chest tightened. What sufferings in this woman's life had driven her to embrace a sorry-looking box filled with small rodents? True, neither of them had permission to enter a chamber not their own, but did that license her to crush this woman's spirit? Both options seemed wrong.

"Please, Miss Chapman." The woman lifted watery eyes to stare into Clara's soul.

Clara fought to keep from flinching. She hated to give in, yet hated to refuse the old lady even more. "Very well, but I should like to go on record as being against this."

The woman's tears vanished, and she darted around Clara. "I'll take this room." She dashed inside and slammed the door.

Clara stared. Had this been some kind of ploy? She turned the question over, examining all sides of it as she wandered down the hall to the next door. Lifting her hand, she rapped on the wood. With any luck, either Ben or Mr. Pocket would answer, freeing her from having to violate whoever's sanctity this room was—yet no one answered. She tried the knob, and the door gave way easily.

Inside, she paused. On a washstand beside the bowl lay a man's shaving mug and brush, along with a straight razor. Next to the bed on a nightstand rested a book, small and leather-bound, with a single red ribbon hanging out, the one Ben had retrieved from the manor's library.

Tingles crawled down her arms, and she rubbed them. This was Ben's room. How indecent of her to have barged in here. What would he think if he found her thus?

She whirled to leave, but remnants of Miss Scurry's cries yet played in her head.

Fine. Better to get this over with while he was still out gathering wood. A cursory look and she could wash her hands of the whole affair. She strode to the center of the room, then dropped to all fours, for surely a mouse would be on such a level.

She searched from wall to wall, floorboard to floorboard. Nothing scampered except the erratic beat of her heart. A fruitless search, but an honest one nonetheless. She could shamelessly tell Miss Scurry she'd given it a good try.

But before giving up and standing, she saw the bedskirt ripple. Could be a draft from the open door or could be the wayward mouse. But which? She swallowed, unsure if she really wanted to find out the truth.

Slowly, she crawled toward the ruffle, then yanked it up, hoping to scare the fellow before it scared her. Nothing but a heap of stained fabric lay there. She sat back on her knees. No mouse. But wait a minute. She bent again and pulled out the garment, then held it up.

Her heart broke when she realized what she held. A prison uniform. Torn. Bloodied. Reeking of sweat and despair. And no doubt belonging to Ben. Heaviness clung to her as if she'd put the garment on her own skin. She could only imagine the indignities he'd suffered. The desire to hold it to her breast and weep warred with the impulse to shove it away.

"Victory!" Miss Scurry's voice rang down the hall.

Clara thrust the horrid garment back beneath the ruffle and fled from the chamber.

The old lady grinned at the other end of the corridor. "Love has returned!"

How on earth had the old lady found the thing? Had she truly lost the mouse in the first place, or had this been some ruse to rifle through rooms she ought not be in? Clara puzzled as she closed the distance between them. Whatever the reason, the sooner they returned downstairs, the better.

"I am happy to hear it." Clara patted the old lady's arm, at the same time guiding her toward the stairs.

"The reckoning is complete, for me at any rate. Oh!" Miss Scurry stopped at the top stair and turned to her, lower lip quivering. "Don't fret, dear. Yours will come as well."

Clara hooked her arm through the old lady's, hopefully urging her onward. She'd not rest until they were at least down on their own bedchambers' floor. "I don't mean to pry, Miss Scurry, but I fear I am not very good at riddles. What is it exactly that you'd hoped to gain by coming here to Bleakly Manor? What was it you were promised?"

"That the lost would be found, dear." Thankfully, the lady grabbed the handrail and worked her way down beside Clara.

"Surely you don't mean your mouse?"

"Oh no, dear." The old lady chuckled. "Though I own I am relieved to have found Love. You see, most people mock me for my special insights, such as Mr. Tallgrass or Mademoiselle Pretents. Others simply ignore me, like Mr. Pocket. But Mr. Minnow was such a gentle soul to me, and then there's you."

They cleared the landing to the second floor, and Miss Scurry turned to her. "Since the moment you arrived, Miss Chapman, you have been the dearest of creatures to me. Why, I'd forgotten how delightful it is to be seen and heard."

Clara licked her lips, still not following the scampering logic of the old woman. "I thank you, but I still don't understand."

"What I lost was my hope in humanity, dear." The old lady patted her arm. "But because of you, I have found it again."

The Seventh Day

DECEMBER 30, 1850

CHAPTER TWENTY

Setting down her plate of cold toast, Clara glanced at the sitting-room door, willing Ben to cross the threshold. A highly irregular chamber in which to eat breakfast, but it was the only room that held any warmth. Despite the blaze in the hearth, she shivered and tugged her shawl tighter at the neck. This manor, these people, were getting to her in a way that crawled under her skin and shimmied across her shoulders. Why had Ben not appeared last night for dinner or for breakfast this morning? Surely by now he'd sent out a letter to every magistrate, barrister, and perhaps every law clerk in the whole of England. It wouldn't do for her to visit his chamber, but she determined then and there that next time the maid Betty entered the room, she'd send her to ask after him.

"Looking at that door will not make your lover arrive any faster." Mademoiselle Pretents's dark eyes needled her from across the room.

A hot trail burned up her neck. Must the woman be so hateful? "Mr. Lane is not my lover."

The woman's lips pulled into a feline smile. "Ahh, but you want him to be, no?"

Near the hearth, Mr. Tallgrass ripped out a crude laugh.

Mr. Pocket rose from his seat and faced the woman, skewering her with a dark look. "Mademoiselle, your coarse innuendos are inappropriate. Besides, how do you know Miss Chapman is not looking for Miss Scurry? That lady has yet to join us this morning as well."

"Pah! *Stupidé* man. What do you know of ladies? Nothing, I tell you." She turned in her seat, murmuring more epithets beneath her breath and ending with a foul assessment at his failure to find her missing jewels.

Picking at a bit of something in his teeth, Mr. Pocket retreated and sat beside Clara on the settee. "I am sorry you must endure such language."

She turned to him, a sheepish smile quirking her lips. "Thank you, Inspector. But I confess I have been watching for Mr. Lane."

Leaning back against the cushions, Mr. Pocket folded his arms. "I wouldn't worry if I were you, miss. Perhaps he's just having a good lie-in this cold morning." The inspector's eyes widened. "Well, well. Speak of the devil and he doth appear."

Heedless of what Mademoiselle Pretents might think or say, Clara's gaze shot to the door—and she gasped. A scabby gouge ran from Ben's brow to his temple. Deep purple spread out in splotches to his eye. An awful, ugly injury. One that might've taken his sight. Or his life.

She flew to his side. "Are you all right?"

"A little mishap, but don't fret." He smirked. "I've seen worse."

No doubt he had, and the thought stung her eyes with tears. Gently, she pushed back his hair for a better look. Sweet mercy. There was nothing little about this. "What happened?"

Ben pulled her hand away and whispered, "All eyes are upon us."

Indeed. She could feel the sharp stab of Mademoiselle Pretents's gaze in her back. Of course Ben wouldn't give her any details. There was no way to have an unmolested conversation in here.

She retreated a step. "I am happy you are accounted for, but I wonder about Miss Scurry. She's usually the first one to breakfast. You didn't happen to see her on your way down?"

"I did not, but that determined look in your eye tells me I shall not rest until I have checked on her for you." He wheeled about and left as quietly as he'd arrived.

"Not without me." Clara followed.

So did Mademoiselle Pretents's voice. "That's right, chase him like the little puppy dog you are."

She tried to ignore the woman and then the lion in the foyer, but both managed to slip beneath her guard, prickling and uncomfortable. Hurrying on, she caught up to Ben on the stairs. "What really happened to you?"

He shrugged. "Yesterday, chopping wood, the inspector's blade flew off and caught me in the head. Had I not turned when I did, well, I have God alone to thank for that."

Lifting her gaze to the heavens as they climbed the stairs, she breathed out, "Amen to that." Then she peered up at Ben. "I was concerned when you didn't appear for dinner and said as much to Mr. Pocket, but he told me you'd said something about attending to business. I assumed that meant writing more letters. I had no idea you'd been injured. Why would he keep that to himself?"

"I don't know." At the top of the stairs he paused and kneaded a muscle at the back of his neck. "And I don't like it."

She caught up to him. "Oh Ben, are you all right? Truly?"

"A bit of head banger, but I'll live. When I returned yesterday afternoon, I lay down for only a moment, or so I thought. Next thing I knew, the sun was up." He smiled down at her. "Forgive me?"

"Of course."

"Then let us check on Miss Scurry." He pivoted and strode to the old lady's chamber. Lifting a fist, he rapped on the wood. "Miss Scurry? Are you in there?"

No answer.

Stepping aside, he allowed Clara to advance and knock.

"Miss Scurry, are you well?"

Nothing.

Reaching past her, Ben tried the knob, and the door opened. "After you. We don't want to frighten the lady if she's abed."

Holding her breath, Clara padded in, afraid of what she might find. What if the old lady had passed during the night and was cold and grey beneath her counterpane? She forced her gaze to land on the bed.

But the covers were untouched, with nary a wrinkle.

"Over here." Ben stood at a curio near the window, holding out a small, sealed envelope. "For you."

Her? She retrieved the missive, and sure enough, *Miss Chapman* was written in shaky cursive. Breaking the seal, she withdrew a small note.

"What does it say?" Ben's voice rumbled behind her.

As she read, warmth spread in her chest, as much from the closeness of the man behind her as from Miss Scurry's sweet words.

"She got what she came for," she murmured as she read. "And she feels no need to remain any longer. She left early this morning."

"But that makes no sense."

"Surprisingly, it does." She folded the note and turned, face-to-face with Ben. "Miss Scurry told me yesterday that I had restored her hope in humanity, all because of my kindness. And that was what she'd lost. Her hope."

Ben stared deep into her eyes, never once varying his gaze. Slowly, he raised his hand and brushed his fingers along her cheek.

Her heart took off, the beat so deafening, surely he could hear it.

"You bring light and air where there is none." His throat bobbed, and a small groan rumbled low. Some kind of war waged behind his stormy gaze, frightful yet alluring, as if he wrestled with—

His mouth came down on hers.

And a thousand suns exploded. He tasted of a summer day, all warmth and promise, and she melted against him. Fire licked along every nerve, birthing a hunger for more. Running her hands up his back, she pressed closer. They'd kissed before, proper and polite, but not like this. Never like this.

Closing her eyes, she surrendered, giving in to a need she never knew existed. His mouth traveled along her jaw and down her neck, until her legs trembled and she could hardly stand. A tremor shook through him as well.

Then he pulled away, chest heaving.

And for some odd reason, her world fell apart. Loss cut sharp. Such passion, once savored, was impossible to walk away from so easily. Lifting a shaky hand to her mouth, she pressed her fingers against lips that felt full and hot.

"Clara, I—" There was an edge to his voice. Primal and raw. He raked his fingers through his hair, breathing hard.

Then he wheeled about and stalked from the room.

How long she stood there, staring at the empty door, she couldn't say. There was only one thing she was sure of. This new Ben was different from the former.

And she wasn't entirely sure what to think about that.

The Eighth Day
DECEMBER 31, 1850

CHAPTER TWENTY-ONE

Sidestepping Mademoiselle Pretents, who stood with hands out-stretched to the hearth, Ben wound his way across the sitting room. How she'd managed to oust Tallgrass from the spot was anybody's guess, though Ben suspected her forked tongue could prod a lame oxen to move along. But besides her continual grousing, events of the day had stretched into an uneventful New Year's Eve. A blessing, that, for his head still ached from the strafing by the ax.

And he wasn't sure he'd ever forget that kiss.

Shoving the thought away, he closed in on the sideboard and dipped the ladle into the punch bowl. This late into the evening, the wassail had chilled, but even so, the spicy scent of cinnamon and cloves wafted up. Outside, wind rattled against the panes, begging for entrance.

"It is a rather dreary New Year's Eve." Behind him, Clara's sweet voice tempered the clattering windows. "Shall we play a game?"

"What's it to be, then?" Mr. Tallgrass snorted. "Blind Man's Buff? Sardines? No, I've got it. How about a relay? A real sweat breaker of a mad dash. Give Jilly the race of her life."

"I–I didn't mean. . .I mean, I didn't think. . ." Clara faltered, her words dying a slow death.

Glass in hand, Ben turned from the table and impaled Tallgrass to his wheeled chair with a glower. "I am certain Miss Chapman meant no insult to you, sir. There are other games besides those requiring physical ability."

"Charades didn't turn out so well." The inspector set a figurine back onto a shelf, either satisfied he'd memorized the details of it or as bored as they all were. Mademoiselle Pretents whirled from the hearth and billowed over to the game table. She yanked out a drawer, then held up a deck of cards. "Come over here. All of you. Let us play Five Card Loo. Everyone has money, no? It is New Year's Eve, after all. Maybe I can earn back the value of my stolen jewels."

Gripping the glass so tightly it might shatter, Ben delivered the wassail to Clara. He was unwilling to admit no money weighted his pockets, though surely everyone suspected as much.

Clara smiled up at him. "Thank you."

He studied her as she took a sip. Her raven hair shone blue-black in the glow of lamplight. Her dress, while nothing as grand as she once wore, fit against her curves in a way that bewitched. He stifled a smirk. No, it wasn't bad luck at all that he didn't have any money, for he was here, with her, a far better lot than rotting in a ship's hold on the way to Australia.

Mr. Tallgrass rumbled in his chair. "Listen, you French witch, if I had any capital, then I wouldn't be here, now would I?"

Setting down her glass of punch, Clara searched in her pocket and pulled out a small silk pouch. Coins tinkled as she poured them into her palm and fingered through them.

Ben narrowed his eyes. What was she up to?

She crossed over to Mr. Tallgrass and held out a half farthing.

The man sneered, his gaze bouncing between the coin and Clara. "What's this?"

"A gift, sir." Her smile shamed them all. "To ward off poverty and misfortune this coming year."

Tallgrass snaked out a hand and snatched it from her, testing the metal of the coin with his teeth. Satisfied, he tucked it away with a grunt. "Fine. Right fine."

Whirling, she padded back to Ben, and his breath hitched. Did ever a purer soul walk the earth? He reached for her hand and gave it a squeeze. "He's right, you know."

Her nose scrunched, the little creases adding to her charm.

"That was a *right fine* thing you did," he explained.

She pulled away, then pressed a coin into his palm, shaking her head to ward off his refusal. "May you have a blessed new year, as well."

He swallowed against the tightness in his throat. "May we both," he whispered.

The first chime of midnight bonged low and resonant. Lacing his fingers with hers, he thanked God with each successive strike of the hour. Not the New Year's he'd expected, but expectations were a realm one ought not dwell in for long.

"A very merry new year to all." Mr. Pocket's voice was a benediction on the echo of the last chime. "A toast is in order, I think."

Smiling, Clara let go of Ben's hand and bent to retrieve her glass. He snagged one of his own, and the unlikely group all lifted their wassail.

"To the master of the manor and the winner of the prize, whomever that may be." The inspector's gaze slid from one person to the next, settling on Ben, then narrowed, his eyes nearly disappearing behind his big nose.

Mademoiselle Pretents tossed back her drink. Spinning, she threw her glass into the hearth, shattering the strange moment. "So, are we going to play some cards or not?"

Tallgrass sucked air in through his teeth. "A half farthing ain't gonna go far, but I never could pass up a good game o' Loo. Shove me over there, girl."

The inspector turned to Clara. "This may be a bit beneath your standards, miss. No shame in retiring now." Then he elbowed Ben as he passed by on his way to the table. "Come on, Lane. We can take the pair of them down."

Clara's gaze followed the man. Then she peered up at Ben. "Indeed. It has been a long day. Stay, if you like, for I bid you good night."

She turned and exited before he could argue the point, which perhaps was a good thing. Had he seen her to her room, the beast inside him might not have stayed leashed after another kiss.

"Will you stand like a lovesick steer, or shall I deal you in, eh?" Mademoiselle Pretents's voice pelted him in the back like grapeshot.

Such coarseness didn't deserve a response, but a retort perched on his tongue nonetheless. He opened his mouth—then as quickly shut it and squatted. There, on the carpet, lay a coin where Clara had stood. Gold. Ancient. He snatched it up and chased after her. She was halfway up the stairs by the time he gained the first step. "Clara, you dropped your special coin."

She smiled over her shoulder. "La! Silly me. I should take better care—"

Her foot shot out. Her arms flailed. She plummeted backward. If her head cracked the wood—

No!

He bolted ahead, taking the stairs two at a time. *Oh, God, help me reach her.*

Arms outstretched, he lunged upward and caught her. Barely. Widening his stance, he hefted them both upright, then leaned her back against the railing for support. Other than being wide-eyed and making little strangling sounds, she appeared to be whole.

He peered closer. "You all right?"

She gulped, then nodded slowly. "Yes, thanks to you. But if you hadn't been here—" All colour drained from her face.

"Thank God I was." Indeed. *Thank You, God.* He tucked back a loosened wisp of her hair, and she trembled beneath his touch—or more likely from the horror of nearly breaking her neck. He held out his arm. "Come on, let's get you to your room."

Her fingers dug into his sleeve, grasping for dear life, and no wonder, for so close had she come to losing hers. Blast those long skirts and feminine frivolities such as lace hems and—what on earth?

He transferred her grasp from his arm to the railing. "Wait here."

Three steps beyond where they stood, the carpet runner bled over onto the lower tread. Crouching, he dissected the step. No wonder Clara had lost her balance.

Someone had removed the brass rod holding the carpet in place.

The Ninth Day

JANUARY 1, 1851

CHAPTER TWENTY-TWO

The next day, Clara stood at the sitting-room window, peering out at a landscape smothered by a fresh coating of snow. Clouds, gravid with possibility, threatened to unleash more of the same. A frozen world wrapped tight in ice and cold—or death, should one venture outside unprepared. The thought prickled gooseflesh along her arms, and she rubbed them absently, praying all the while that Aunt was keeping warm.

"You hardly touched your breakfast this morning. Not that I blame you. I ate better at Millbank."

Ben's deep voice warmed her from behind, and she turned from the glass, letting the sheer fall back into place. He stood so close that she breathed in his scent of pine soap, tangy as a woodland forest. His gaze, hinting at unchecked emotion, made her forget about the wintry world outside. Ahh, but she could get used to spending all her days with this man.

He held out his hand. "I've brought you something." A small golden scone rested atop his palm.

"Where did you find that?" Regardless of his answer, she took the morsel from him, lips already moistened in anticipation.

He cocked a brow while she devoured the treat. "Surely you don't expect me to reveal all my secrets, hmm?"

Outside the closed doors of the sitting room, men's voices grew louder. A few good-natured shouts. Some laughter. Had the master of the manor finally arrived now, on New Year's Day? She peered up at Ben.

He swept out his hand. "After you."

Mademoiselle Pretents beat them to the threshold, sliding the doors open wide, with Mr. Pocket at her heels. Mr. Tallgrass merely grumbled in his wheeled chair, requesting Jilly to once more straighten him.

"What is this?" Mademoiselle Pretents marched into the foyer. By the time Clara and Ben caught up, crimson crept in ever-widening patches on the lady's cheeks.

"It is not fair to add more to our number with only six days remaining. *Non!*" She stamped her foot, the clack of it resounding on the marble tile. "I will not have it. You hear me?"

"Mademoiselle"—Mr. Pocket leaned toward her—"I do not think it is up to you."

"Pah!" She whirled and stalked back into the sitting room, her grey skirt as puffed up as she was.

Near the front door, Betty, the petite maid who'd fretted over the Boxing Day incident, held out her arms, collecting all manner of brightly coloured hats and scarves and coats. Three men, lithe and lean, continued to add to her pile so that soon it grew to her chin. Any more and she'd go down.

The tallest man of the trio turned to them. "Greetings to you, fine residents of Bleakly Manor. We are the Brothers Penfold." He lifted to his toes and flourished his arm out to his side.

The two others, identically blue eyed and freckled of face, pranced forward with precise steps, lining up in a neat row.

"Dawson at your service." The first one dipped a bow.

"Lawson at your service." The second folded as well.

Mr. Pocket held out his hand, stopping them, and faced the tallest of the men. "Let me guess. You're Clawson."

The man laughed, his shaggy red hair sweeping his collar with the movement. "A valiant effort, but no. Charles, at your service." He bowed so low, his head nearly hit the floor.

Then the three of them snapped into action, tumbling and balancing and leaping into more gymnastics than were feasible in the foyer. All the while, they chanted:

"We come to bring you cheer,
for a very merry new year,
with song, and dance, and rhyme,
for a splendidly wonderful time.
We are the Brothers Penfold!"

The twin men clasped hands and raised them high, while the taller man, Charles, dove beneath the arc and somersaulted to a stop in front of Clara. He captured her hand and brought it to his mouth, pressing his lips against her skin.

She gasped.

Ben stepped closer to her side. She couldn't see, but if she dared a peek, no doubt his hands were fisted.

Charles winked up at her, then jumped to his toes. "My good people, your entertainment begins in an hour. Don't be late."

He pivoted and joined his brothers. As one, the three of them snatched up their bags and turned to the overburdened servant. "Lead on, my fair maiden," Charles said. "For we shall need time to prepare."

Mr. Pocket's gaze followed the retreating performers. "Interesting turn of events, I'd say."

Ben said nothing. He merely ushered Clara into the sitting room with a light touch to the small of her back.

For the next hour, each tick of the clock seemed to go slower, especially with Mademoiselle Pretents working herself into a frenzy. Despite Clara's best efforts at calming her, the lady bristled about the addition of three more people to compete for the prize.

After an eternity, Betty appeared in the doorway. "The Brothers Penfold request your audience in the drawing room."

"Flap and rubbish! I'll freeze me rumpus off in there." Mr. Tallgrass's lips twisted into a sour pout. "Why can't the blasted fellows come in here?"

Betty clasped her hands in front of her, and Clara knew the frustration she must be feeling. They all wanted to strangle the words from Mr. Tallgrass by now.

"Please," Betty continued. "If you would follow me."

Tugging her shawl tight at the neck, Clara huddled close to Ben on their way out. As much as she hated to admit it, Mr. Tallgrass's sentiments were correct. It would be cold away from the sitting-room hearth.

The hallway portraits stared like living creatures. She could feel them measuring and judging each one of them. Clara shivered. What a horrid thought. But the quiver melted as Ben escorted her into the drawing room.

No new draperies had yet been hung since the Christmas tree incident, but even without thick fabric on the windows, the chamber was as warm as a late spring day. A huge fire burned on the grate and appeared to have been lit for quite some time. Why had Betty not suggested they move their party into this room sooner?

"Have a seat, gentlefolk, and let the merriment begin." Charles waggled his fingers at four chairs lined up in front of a cleared area on the carpet. Then he disappeared behind a curtain hung from a frame.

Clara stared, wide-eyed. When had they time to construct that?

"Roll me over, Jilly," Mr. Tallgrass commanded.

The girl put all her weight into shoving the big toady toward the row of chairs.

Mademoiselle Pretents jumped back as Jilly careened too close to the woman's skirts. "*Stupidé* girl!"

Ben shook his head and led Clara to the seats on the farthest side, placing himself between her and Mr. Pocket.

Lawson, or maybe it was Dawson, strutted out first. Dressed in all black, the only coloured things about him were his shock of red hair, painted white face, and white gloves. The other twin followed, and they bent low, making way for Charles, who entered bearing a sign that read News of the Realm ~ A Silent Review of 1850.

Clara smiled up at Ben. He smiled back with an arch to his brow, and her heart warmed. So, he'd remembered. Pantomimes were her favorite sort of entertainment.

Without a word, the actors parodied an important event for each month from the past year, from the creation of the first public library last January, all the way up to December and the death of some banker.

A banker? Clara cocked her head. Not that a man's death wasn't important, but who was the fellow?

Mr. Tallgrass startled. "What's that? Who's the money-snatchin' banker what died? Act that out, ye blimey stooges."

Lawson and Dawson dramatized the man's name, but by the time they made it to the last syllable of the last name, Mr. Tallgrass pitched forward in his chair, practically spilling onto the floor.

"Flap! Bayham Bagstock is dead you say? Oh, that's rich. That's more 'n rich." Mr. Tallgrass laughed so hard, his breath wheezed and moisture ran from his nose and eyes. He tilted dangerously to one side.

"Oy me rumpus! Jilly, lend a hand."

Clara exchanged a glance with Ben, who shrugged, as much at a loss as her.

"Mr. Tallgrass, are you quite all right?" she asked. "Did you know this Mr. Bagstock?"

"More 'n right, I'd say. Turn me around, girl." Jilly shoved him so that his chair faced them instead of the players, who now stood watching the show put on by the guests.

Mr. Tallgrass grinned. A rare occurrence—in fact it was the only time Clara could remember ever seeing his teeth exposed in a truly pleasurable fashion. "Mr. Bayham Bagstock is the bugger what's been squashing me beneath his greedy thumb. Now that he's kicked off, there's no more Bagstocks to hound me, not a one. That's what's what and what's right. I'm free!" His shoulders shook with another peal of laugher. "Jilly! Get me rumpus out here. We're done with this mad house."

Scowling, the girl leaned her weight into the chair, wheeling him across the carpet and out the door.

"Good riddance." Mademoiselle Pretents shifted in her seat and looked down her nose at them. "That *imbécile* was getting on my nerves."

Clara pressed her lips tight, trapping a retort behind her teeth.

Mr. Pocket sniffed, his enormous nose bobbing with the force of it. "It seems our number is dwindling, by design or by accident."

Accident? Next to her, Ben snorted, and she would, too, were she not a lady. There was nothing accidental about anything related to Bleakly Manor.

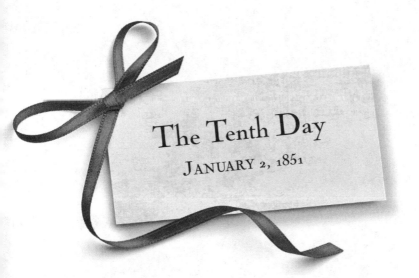

The Tenth Day

JANUARY 2, 1851

CHAPTER TWENTY-THREE

The tallest Penfold wrapped his multicoloured scarf around his neck with a flourish, and Ben widened his stance on the foyer tiles, resisting the urge to help the brothers out the door more quickly.

Next to him, Clara squeezed his arm and whispered, "Patience is a virtue."

He quirked a half smile down at her. "Whatever gave you the impression I was virtuous?"

Despite their thick wraps, the three Penfolds backflipped, then lowered to one knee, aligned in a row in front of the door. "*Adieu*, good gentles," they said in unison.

"Pah!" Mademoiselle Pretents whirled toward the sitting room. "Good-bye, silly men."

Lawson and Dawson rose to their toes and pirouetted. Charles somersaulted to a stop in front of Clara.

Oh no. Not again. Ben sidestepped between the man and Clara. "Godspeed on your journey, Mr. Penfold."

A rogue grin spread across Charles's face, and he rose to join his brothers. "A blessed new year to one and all."

The three dipped a bow, then slipped out into the waiting arms of a January morning. By the time the door closed, a blast of air embraced Ben and Clara as well.

She huddled a step closer to him. "They were merry fellows, were they not?"

His mouth twisted. "Perhaps a little too merry."

"I am sorry to see them leave. At least they were a diversion." She sighed, as if the weight of so many days inside the bleak walls could no longer be contained. "My mending basket is nearly empty, and I confess I shall scream if I must spend another day listening to the mademoiselle badger the inspector for a lead on her missing jewels."

Ben rubbed out a kink at the back of his neck. Just thinking of the harping woman tightened his muscles. "Nor do I wish to write any more letters. By now I've canvassed every lawgiver in all of England." He blew out a sigh and smiled at Clara. "What say we go for a stroll? I've a new appreciation for fresh air."

She hugged herself. "It's rather cold outside."

He glanced at the front door, wishing for a good leg stretcher, but indeed, hoarfrost crept around the edges of the frame. He turned to Clara and offered his arm. "All right. We shall have an adventure indoors."

She gaped. "Do you think we should? I mean, what if the master of the manor finally arrives, only to find us nosing about his home?"

The shrill voice of Mademoiselle Pretents pestering Mr. Pocket couldn't have been timed better. Ben nodded toward the sitting room.

Clara grabbed his arm. "Adventure, here we come."

Before passing beneath the lion head, Ben veered left, taking them down a corridor he'd seen only the servants use. Before long, shadows closed in, and he retraced their steps back to the foyer.

Clara arched a brow at him. "That was a quick adventure."

Opening a drawer in the trestle table, he retrieved a vigil candle in a glass, lit the wick, and set off again.

Clara matched her steps to his, and that simple action caused an ache deep in his chest. Despite all the wretched treachery of the past year, and yes, even her betrayal at losing faith in him, his heart still yearned to make her his own.

But what did he have to offer her other than the status of a convict? He clenched his jaw to keep from grinding his teeth, determination to find who did this to him—to her—pumping a fresh rage through his veins with each step.

"Have you heard from any of the solicitors or barristers yet?" Clara's sweet voice pulled him back from such abysmal thoughts.

"No. I'm beginning to think my attempts to contact the outside world are being thwarted. That the desk set up in my chamber is nothing but a ruse and the stable boy isn't delivering any of the letters."

"To what end?"

He paused in front of a narrow door and shook his head. "Perhaps

I'm being too cynical."

Trying the knob, he shoved the door open, expecting it would lead to a servants' stair. Daylight flooded into the corridor, blinding him for a moment. Blinking, he strode into the room.

"I don't blame you." Clara trailed him. "This is a curious situation."

Inside the chamber, Ben's shoes sank into plush carpeting. A hearth fire burned warm and inviting. A bed, rumpled bedclothes atop it, was to his left, and a small library lined the opposite wall. Writing pens, nibs, parchments, and bottles of ink inhabited every possible horizontal surface. He inhaled, dissecting the air. The smoky scent of Bright Leaf tobacco mixed with the spicy aroma of fine wine, possibly an aged Bordeaux, if he wasn't mistaken. Did the master himself reside in this small chamber?

Clara grasped his sleeve. "We don't belong here. Please, let's leave."

He patted her hand and led them out, taking care to close the door exactly as it had been. In the murk of the corridor, he winked at her, hoping to soothe her fears. "I promised you adventure, did I not?"

She swatted his arm.

Turning, he led them down the rest of the hall, Clara's fingers digging into his arm all the while. If he didn't put her mind at ease, his exploring would be put to an end before he could discover exactly who dwelt in this wing.

"Any news of your aunt?" he asked.

"No, but I suppose no news is good news. Perhaps she is on the mend."

He smiled down at her. "One would hope."

The corridor ended at another door. This time he rapped on it first, just in case it wasn't a stair—and if it wasn't, if a gentleman answered, what ought he say?

Clara grasped his arm with two hands, jostling the candle so that the light guttered. "I think I should prefer Mademoiselle Pretents's badgering to this. Let's go back."

He tried the knob. Locked.

"Ben!"

Ignoring Clara's protests, he pressed his ear against the wood and listened. Only Clara's quickened breaths filled the small space. He'd have to investigate the possibility another time.

Turning his back to the mystery, he offered her a half smile and led her the other way. "So, I take it you've not heard from your brother, either?"

"No, not since he sailed."

Strange, that. Why would a brother, so close to his family, not send word of a safe arrival after traveling the expanse of an ocean? He held the candle higher and glanced at Clara. "Then how do you know that's truly where he went?"

Her brow dipped. "What do you mean?"

"Just that your faith in him is unrivaled." He forced the words out smoothly, struggling to keep the bitterness raging inside from rushing out. Would that she'd have had that much confidence in him.

"I should think as his partner those many years at Blythe, working together for the good of the company, you'd have faith in him as well. Mr. Blythe certainly did, or he'd not have considered George for partnership. But you know this. So why question my brother's whereabouts? George lost his livelihood the very same day you lost yours."

"No, he didn't." He stopped and turned to her. This close to where the corridor opened up to the front foyer, light poured in so that he could read her face. "You said yourself that a week passed before he was summoned by the solicitor."

"Oh, Ben." She rested her palm on his cheek, the touch so intimate, so familiar, it almost drove him to his knees. "I know you want to find out who did this to you, to us, but my brother cannot be to blame. Lay such logic to rest, if for no other reason than for me."

He averted his gaze, looking at anything but the violet pleading in her eyes. Of course he didn't want to blame his friend, his colleague, but the timing of everything was off. And if—hold on. What the devil?

Candlelight caught on a gap in the paneling just beyond Clara. Sidestepping her, he ran his fingers along the edge.

"What are you doing?" she asked.

A nudge, followed by a shoulder shove, opened a small door, just wide enough for him to edge through sideways.

Clara grabbed his coat hem. "Do you think that's safe?"

"Wait here. I'll find out." Narrow stairs forced him to cross foot over foot. A dark ascent, impossible without the candle.

"What is it?" Clara's voice called from below. "What's up there?"

"Looks like. . ." The stairs ended, and he held the candle out in front of him. A remnant of Bright Leaf tobacco wafted like a ghost in the darkness.

"Ben?"

"It's a crawl space," he called down.

Crouch-walking, he worked his way along a thick timber, the walls barely wide enough for his shoulders. Ahead, a beam of light pulled him forward, not brilliant, but enough to indicate it leaked in from somewhere. He pressed on and stopped where a large circle had been cut into the plaster. Beyond the circle was a shadowy depression with two smaller holes at center and a larger one below. Cautiously, he leaned forward, putting his head into the tiny cave, and peered out the two gaps.

Below him was the foyer. The front door straight ahead. The sitting room to the left. A view that could only be seen from one angle.

The lion's head.

The Eleventh &
Twelfth Days
JANUARY 3–4, 1851

CHAPTER TWENTY-FOUR

Tucking her needle case back into her sewing basket, Clara glanced at the mantel clock as it chimed. Then frowned. Both Mademoiselle Pretents and Ben had disappeared after breakfast—five hours ago. Now that she'd caught up with her mending, she'd have to invent something else to bide her time.

Across the room, Mr. Pocket gazed at her over the top of the book he'd been reading. "Looking at the clock will not make Mr. Lane appear any faster, you know."

Her face heated from his assessment, yet how could she not help but fret? Ever since discovering that locked door yesterday, Ben had been dead set on revisiting the area. She'd held him off, but apparently not for good—none of which was Mr. Pocket's business.

She straightened her skirts, smoothing her palms along her thighs. "I could just as easily be waiting for Mademoiselle Pretents."

"Could be." He rubbed a hand over his shorn head, the peppery bristles shushing with his touch, then ended by working a muscle in his neck. "But that pretty blush on your cheeks says otherwise."

She averted her gaze, suddenly preferring the burning embers in the hearth to the questions igniting the inspector's brown eyes. How to turn this around? She bit her lip and—that was it. Turn it around, back onto him.

She flashed him a smile. "Have you never been in love, Inspector?"

"As a matter of fact." He set down his book and leaned forward, hands dangling between his knees. "There's a certain woman I intend on courting very soon. Tell me, Miss Chapman, have you any advice on the matter?"

Leaving her sewing basket behind, she crossed the rug to take a seat adjacent to his. "Does the lady return your affections, sir?"

"She does." Mr. Pocket scratched at his side-whiskers before continuing. "Her father, however, is another matter altogether."

"I am sorry to hear that. You seem a fine-enough fellow."

"Thank you, miss. I like to think so."

The melancholy twist of the man's mouth tugged at her heart. He wasn't a dashing figure, to be sure, but neither were his garments threadbare. She looked closer. A ruddy complexion, but no pockmarks. Teeth somewhat stained, yet all present. Clearly he was a capable man, as evidenced by his keen mind and hale body. She tapped a finger on her skirt as she further evaluated him but came up empty-handed. "What is the problem, sir, if I may be so bold?"

"I wish I could say it wasn't money." Furrows creased his brow. "But it always seems to boil down to that, does it not?"

"Indeed." A bitter taste soured the back of her throat. She'd personally experienced all too well how lack of funding and social status turned away those she'd thought were friends. She swallowed and focused instead on the man in front of her. "But surely you make a sustainable living as an officer of the law?"

He nodded. "I'm comfortable enough, but it's not so much the jingle in my pocket. It's more than that. All the trimmings and show of society concern her father the most. He'll see her live nowhere but in a fine London town house." A shadow darkened his face, sinister and almost demonic. "As if Clapham wasn't good enough."

Clara edged back in her seat.

Then just as suddenly, his eyes cleared, and he smiled at her. "Not to worry, though. In three days' time, all will be remedied. I've put a deposit on just such a town house already."

Alarm tightened her tummy, and she pressed her hand to it. How did he know he'd be the one to receive the prize?

"Was that not a bit premature?" she asked.

His dark eyes pinned her in place. "Not if I can pay it off before mid-January."

"But what if you cannot?"

"Then I lose everything."

Her jaw dropped. "Mr. Pocket, do you think that was a very wise act?"

"Sometimes one must act boldly to bring about a bold hope."

"Or a bold failure," she whispered under her breath.

He leaned forward. "What's that?"

"Nothing." She forced a smile and glanced once more at the clock, longing for the sanctuary of Ben's presence. "I wish you the best with your lady, Mr. Pocket."

"Thank you. I believe you mean that, and as such, I am almost sorry my gain will mean your loss."

She shot her gaze back to his. "What do you mean?"

"Thief!" A grey storm cloud blew through the sitting-room door. Mademoiselle Pretents marched over and planted her feet in front of the Inspector—a gun in her hand. "You are *ze* one who stole my jewels. No wonder you could not tell me who took them."

Sucking in a breath, Clara shrank into the chair, putting as much space as possible between her and the crazed woman.

Mr. Pocket merely chuckled. "You are confused, mademoiselle. I operate on the right side of the law."

"Liar!" The woman's voice shook. So did the gun. "Give them to me."

All mirth faded from Mr. Pocket's face, replaced by the same disturbing shadow of moments before. "Put the gun down. Now."

"I will not! I will have my jewels or shoot you like the dog you are." Her voice rose to a screech. "You think I won't use this? Give me the jewel pouch."

With each quiver of the gun's muzzle, Clara's heart beat harder, seeking escape, as did she. She crept to the edge of her seat, debating if the woman would allow her to leave unharmed.

Mr. Pocket reached inside his dress coat.

And whipped out a gun of his own.

Two shots exploded. So did Mr. Pocket's chest. His pistol dropped from his hand, and he flew back against the cushions with a curse. Blood oozed out the torn fabric of his waistcoat. His hand slammed to his chest as he tried to staunch the flow. Red oozed between his fingers.

Clara stared, unable to stop a scream.

The gun barrel swung her way.

"Shut up, *lay-dee*, or you are next."

CHAPTER TWENTY-FIVE

Two shots rang out, violating the solemn January afternoon. Ben jerked away from exploring the drawing room and ran to the door, listening with his whole body. The gunshot was nearby. Definitely on this floor. Down the hall. Likely the sitting room.

A scream next. Clara's.

His heart skipped a beat—then he bolted down the corridor. *Oh God, please.*

Just before the door, he forced his feet to a standstill. Every muscle quivered to race in and sweep Clara away from danger, but he'd be no use to her with a bullet through his own head.

Holding his breath, he peered around the doorframe.

And his heart stopped.

Across the room, Mademoiselle Pretents aimed a gun at Clara. Nearby, the inspector slumped against the settee cushion, bleeding.

If that French hothead pulled the trigger again—

Shoving the consequences out of his mind, Ben yanked off his shoe and threw it at the window behind the woman.

Glass shattered.

Mademoiselle Pretents whirled toward the sound.

He strode through the door.

The woman jerked her face toward him, gun barrel trained on his chest. Excellent. Better at him than at Clara.

"*Homme fou!*" The grey menace spit out a host of curses. "Why you do that?"

He held up his hands, appearing to surrender, but continued walking. Smooth steps. Slow. If he could keep her talking long enough to draw close, he stood a greater chance of disarming her.

Unless she shot him first.

"I merely wanted to get your attention." He spoke as to a wee child on the verge of a tantrum. "What's going on in here?"

Across the room, Clara whimpered. Mr. Pocket eked out a painful grunt.

Ben kept walking. Five more paces, and he'd be in range to snatch the gun.

Mademoiselle Pretents's dark eyes rooted on him, murder glinting. "This is none of your concern."

He nodded toward the revolver. "Looks like you just made it mine."

Three more steps.

She straightened her arm like a ramrod, the muzzle jutting closer to him. "Stop! Or I will shoot."

He took another step.

A strangled cry garbled from Clara's throat.

"I told you to shut up, *lay-dee*!" Mademoiselle Pretents yelled.

One pace more. So close.

"She means you no harm, mademoiselle, nor do I." He raised his hands higher, shoulder level, and dared a final step. "Do you have a quarrel with me?"

She opened her mouth—

He shot out his left hand, grabbing the top of the barrel. His right hand snapped into the tender flesh of her inner wrist. The momentum directed the muzzle toward her belly, and she let go.

Transferring the revolver to his right hand, he aimed it at her. "Not so nice to be on the other end, is it?"

Wine-coloured blotches darkened her cheeks. French indictments thickened the air, along with vile names directed at him and Mr. Pocket.

"Clara"—he spoke without varying his gaze—"fetch me a stocking from your mending basket."

Keeping a wide berth from the Frenchwoman, Clara stole over to her basket and retrieved a long silken legging. Perfect.

He tipped his head toward the seat Clara had recently vacated. "Sit in that chair, mademoiselle."

"You are a devil!" She grumbled all the way to her seat, then plopped down, her skirts ballooning like a rain cloud. "I am not the criminal here. He is!" Her evil eye speared Pocket through the heart.

"He stole my jewels, I tell you."

Before tying up the woman, Ben glanced at the inspector. A little pale, but not deathly. The heel of his hand kept pressure on the wound, upper right chest, near the shoulder. Blood soaked through his shirt and waistcoat, but not in a pulsing stream. It wasn't a killing shot, unless infection set in. He'd need attention soon, though.

First to secure the French firebrand. Turning his back to the inspector, Ben traded the gun for the stocking in Clara's hand. Worried eyes peered deeply into his. She'd likely never held a revolver in her life.

Mademoiselle Pretents started to rise.

Ben pushed her back. He tied each of her hands tightly to the chair arms. While he worked, the woman called down all manner of fiery oaths upon his head, his mother, and any future children he might sire. Finally, he fumbled with the knot of his cravat and freed his tie, then shoved the fabric into her mouth. The woman's eyes widened an instant before tapering to angry slashes.

For the first time in an eternity, he breathed deeply, pulse finally slowing.

Clara huddled next to him, face drained of colour. "Thank you. If you'd not arrived when you did—"

"Then there would've been one less person for me to deal with." Mr. Pocket's words snarled behind them, followed by the cock of a pistol hammer. "But no matter. I've drawn this out long enough."

Bile seared upward from Ben's gut. The Christmas tree fire. The thinned ice. The flying ax head and the loosened stair carpeting. It all made sense now. Fury quaked through him. Pocket hadn't been sent here to watch him—the man was here to make sure none of them remained.

"Put the gun on the floor, miss. Then turn around and push it to me with your toe. Slowly." Pocket's voice was kicked gravel. From intimidation or pain?

Ben angled his head, listening harder.

"Move one more twitch, Lane, and you're a dead man," Pocket warned.

"Don't worry, Inspector. I've got him covered." The steel in Clara's voice stabbed him through the heart.

He'd taken kidney punches before, sharp enough to stop his breathing, but this time, he doubted he'd ever breathe again. He slid his gaze to the left, where Clara backed away from him.

The gun in her hand aimed at his head.

Chapter Twenty-Six

The revolver shook in Clara's hands, but not from the cold bleeding in from the broken window or from inexperience with firearms. Her brother had seen to that, instructing her in the pursuit of marksmanship when his friends were scarce.

So while the weight and grip molded in her palm was entirely familiar, it was the act of aiming the thing at Ben that caused the muscles in her arms to quiver. Calculating the probability of success for such a wild scheme was impossible. She wrapped her fingers tighter around the grip, heart racing. This *had* to work. It must. Or they'd both be dead.

And Ben would go to his grave thinking the worst of her.

"Hold it right there, missy." Mr. Pocket's pistol, smaller than the revolver in her own hand, wavered ever so slightly between her and Ben. "What are you about?"

She dared one more step back, gaining as much distance from Ben as possible. "I should like to parley, Mr. Pocket."

Mademoiselle Pretents whinnied some kind of comment behind the gag in her mouth.

Ben stiffened, the fabric of his dress coat stretching taut across his shoulders.

God, please, may Ben forgive me. Her stomach twisted. Had she not just minutes before portended Mr. Pocket's bold actions might be a bold failure?

"Parley for what?" Mr. Pocket snorted. "I hold the advantage. You shoot Mr. Lane, and I put a shot through you. There's nothing to negotiate."

"Ahh, but there is." The slight smile curving her lips tasted like rancid fat. But showing fear of any kind would attract a bullet. She lifted her chin. "Allow me to reach into my pocket, sir, for I have something of value to offer you."

Mr. Pocket narrowed his eyes. "In exchange for what?"

"My life."

A curse, foul as any Mademoiselle Pretents had uttered, flew past his lips. "I could just shoot you now and take whatever it is from you."

True, except as she studied the pallor of his skin, the red soaking through not only his waistcoat but his dress coat, she doubted he had much stamina remaining. She lifted her chin higher, looking down her nose at him. "You could, but in so doing Mr. Lane would no doubt attack you. You saw how quickly he moves. Do you really think in your state you'd stand a chance of reloading before he disarmed you? Oh, don't look so surprised, Mr. Pocket. I may be a lady, but I can tell the difference between a pistol and a revolver."

She flashed a glance at Ben. It wasn't much, but would he take the hint?

The smell of blood and curiosity tainted the chill air. Mr. Pocket's mouth twisted while he considered her words, as if he sucked upon a lemon sour.

"All right. What will you trade for your life, Miss Chapman?" he asked.

"A coin, sir. One of great value." She dared tiny steps backward as she spoke, inches really, but every bit of gained ground felt like a small triumph. "And in your current financial state, I believe if you add the coin's worth to the prize offered you as the last remaining guest at Bleakly Manor, your money woes shall be at an end. I give you the coin, and you let me leave the manor unharmed. Now."

Mr. Pocket sniffed, not nearly with as much gusto as usual, though. In fact, his nose barely bobbed at all. "All right. Let's have a look at it before I go making any promises. But so help me, miss, if you pull out anything other than a coin, I shall shoot you just for the pleasure of it."

Without moving his body, Ben arched a brow at her.

She prayed with each heartbeat that the poison of her movements and words would not taint what he knew of her trustworthiness from the past. Withdrawing the second-chance coin, she pinched it between thumb and forefinger and held it up so the weak afternoon sunlight would cause it to gleam.

"Very nice." The inspector narrowed his eyes, his tone lowering to a rumble. "But how do I know that's real?"

For the space of a breath, she glanced at Ben, pleading for understanding with her eyes.

Then she snapped her gaze back to the inspector. "Here. Catch."

She tossed the coin to him.

And Ben wheeled about, diving for the man.

Grunts, curses, and the crack of gunshot.

Then nothing but the crash of a picture frame across the room, smashed to the floor by a bullet gone wild.

Pocket moaned on the settee. For once Mademoiselle Pretents was completely silent.

Ben turned, chest heaving—with naught but a mark on his cheek to show for the scuffle.

Clara lowered her gun. "Thank God."

Ben's eyes burned like blackened embers, searching her from head to hem. "Are you hurt?"

"I am not." Her voice shook, as did her whole body, but other than that she remained whole.

With a nod, Ben turned back to the inspector. Heedless of the man's injury, he yanked open Mr. Pocket's dress coat and rummaged inside.

Mr. Pocket cried out like an animal.

Clara winced, the tender part of her heart competing with the vengeful side.

Ben retrieved a small black velvet pouch. "Like you, Inspector, I never accuse without solid evidence."

Mademoiselle Pretents rocked on her chair, throaty roars fighting to escape the gag in her mouth.

Ben turned on her. "Yet neither do I believe these are your jewels, mademoiselle. The courts will decide on the matter. Clara, ring for the maid, if you please. A constable and a physician are in order, I think."

Crossing to the bell pull near the door, she yanked on the golden rope. Cold air blasted in from the window, and she trembled. What an eventful day. A smirk tugged at her mouth. No, what an eventful holiday. With a sigh, she laid the revolver on the sideboard.

"I cannot believe what you just did." Ben's voice accused her from behind.

She froze, fearful to face him. Would he scold? Rebuke? Be angry that she'd pointed a gun at him? Oh, sweet mercy! One wrong move and she could've accidentally shot him. What had she been thinking?

"Clara."

His husky voice turned her around, and his smile weakened her already shaky knees.

"Well done."

The softness in his gaze tightened her throat, and with the last of her strength, she offered him a frail smile. "Thank you."

He stepped closer, smelling of battle and promise. "With those two out of the picture"—he nodded his head toward the subdued pair across the room—"that leaves just you and me. I'd say we are a brilliant team, are we not?"

"Yes." For a moment, she reveled in the unity, the embrace of his unfettered admiration shining in his eyes.

But then reality slapped her as stinging a blow as the next waft of frigid air. Her smile faded.

Ben reached for her but, inches from contact, pulled back. "What troubles you?"

"A team may not receive the promised prize." She bit her lip, working the fleshy part between her teeth. With Mr. Pocket and Mademoiselle Pretents out of the picture, only she and he were left.

She swallowed. Ought she give up the funds she desperately needed so that he might receive his freedom?

CHAPTER TWENTY-SEVEN

The front door closed on a writhing Mademoiselle Pretents, arm grasped tightly in a constable's grip, and the lagging Mr. Pocket, shored up by the strong hold of a physician. The thud of wood against wood faded in the foyer like the last beat of a heart. Clara rubbed her arms, chilled by the night air creeping across the tiled floor. She ought to be grateful there'd been no need to call an undertaker. And truly she was, but an uneasy pressure that'd been building since the day she arrived dwarfed her gratitude.

Fear. What would happen next? Nothing good, considering the way the lifeless lion eyes burned down from its perch on the wall.

Turning from the door, the maid faced her and Ben. "Will that be all, sir, miss?

Ben nodded. "Yes, Betty. It's late, and tomorrow's a new day. It will do us all well to end this one, I think."

Betty dipped her head. "Yes, sir. Good night, sir. Good night, miss." She scurried past them, the scent of silver polish in her wake.

Clara watched her disappear down the corridor, wondering if the woman would catch a wink of sleep. Would she toil into the witching hours, shining silverware and soup tureens for a nearly nonexistent house party?

"Shall we?" Ben offered his arm. "I'll see you to your room."

She rested her fingers on his sleeve, and he tucked her hand into the crook of his arm. Secure. Warm. A queer tinge rippled in her tummy. Was it safe to hope again?

She peeked up at Ben as they mounted the staircase. "I do feel sorry that neither Mademoiselle nor Mr. Pocket received what they'd come for, and indeed left here with so much less."

"I suppose you could look at it that way."

She studied the strong cut of his jaw, looking for a humorous twitch, but he held it firm.

"What else is there to think?" she asked.

"Well. . ." Ben peered down at her. "Mademoiselle Pretents came here with the hope of a new position in a new household. I'd say she got both, though a cell wasn't likely what she had in mind for accommodations. She is, however, up to the challenge of teaching an entire prison population some new obscenities, in English and in French."

Clara bit her lip to keep from smiling—a nearly impossible task, for the twinkle in his eyes was almost her undoing. "You, sir, arc wicked."

"Perhaps, but I am correct, am I not?" He turned to her at the second-floor landing, longing in his gaze—but longing for what? Approval?

Or for her?

Soft light flickered from the wall sconces, bathing half his face in brightness, the other in shadows. Fitting, really. Nine months ago his very life had been golden one moment, black the next. As had hers.

Ignoring his question, she let go of his arm and reached up, tracing a scar from his temple to cheek, one that narrowly missed his eye.

His skin burned against her touch, his gaze asking questions she wasn't sure she wanted to answer. If she leaned closer, raised to her toes, his mouth would be hers once again. She could be his. No one would know.

Except for God.

The thought sobered her, and she pulled back. "What, uh, what of Mr. Pocket?" She set off down the corridor leading to her chamber and called over her shoulder. "You cannot say he shall be rewarded with a magistrate position."

"True." Ben caught up to her in three long strides. "But he will be spending some very personal time with a magistrate, hmm?"

"That doesn't count, and you know it." She swatted his arm with a grin.

"No, but it did coax a pretty smile from you, which was my intent all along." He winked at her.

She matched her feet to her increased heartbeat, hastening down the hall. Passing Miss Scurry's door, she shivered. Now with

Mademoiselle Pretents absent as well, she'd sleep alone on this floor.

"It's quite empty here without Miss Scurry," she murmured. "As quirky as she was, I do miss the old lady, but not her mice."

"Two more nights. That's all." Ben pulled ahead of her and reached for the knob on her door, opening it for her. "Just two, and I shall have my freedom and you your money."

"That would be breaking the rules."

"After all that's happened these past ten days, do you really think convention is a priority of Bleakly Manor's master?" He ushered her across the threshold with a sweep of his hand. "Now then, there's no need to worry about anything. With Mr. Pocket gone, there will be no more mishaps."

She turned to him. "I hope so."

"I know so." Drawing near, he pressed a light kiss to her forehead, whispering "Sleep well" against her skin.

She stood, dazed, long after he pulled the door shut behind him. Sleeping was out of the question, though she did try eventually. She fought with twisted bedsheets the whole of the night, turning one way and another, until just before dawn when she finally surrendered the battle.

Faint light leached through the windowpanes by the time she opened her door, dressed for whatever the day might bring. But she stopped on the threshold, completely unprepared for the sight in front of her.

Across from her door, Ben slept, back against the wall, legs sprawled, head tipped back, wearing the same clothing as yesterday except for more wrinkles. Peace eased the lines on his face. Each rise and fall of his chest breathed life into the boyish good looks she remembered—so carefree, so handsome that the sight made her ache to the marrow of her bones.

A second later, he shot to his feet, knife drawn, scanning the hall.

Heart pounding, she grabbed the doorframe for support.

"You all right?" He peered past her shoulders, into her chamber.

"Fine, except for the year of life you just frightened from me." She drew in a long breath, slowing her pulse. "What are you doing here?"

He tucked away his knife—thankfully—then ran a hand through his hair. "I told you last night there'd be no more mishaps. I meant it."

Heat spread up from her tummy to her heart. He'd slept in front of her door all night, watching and protecting her?

Down the hall, a bobbing lamp drew near, the halo of light contrasting the maid's pale face with her ebony dress. Betty bobbed a curtsy despite her filled hands. "Glad to see you're both awake. There's a messenger downstairs for Miss Chapman. He said to give this to you directly."

Betty held out an envelope with Clara's name scratched on the front.

Clara's heart stopped. This could not be good. With shaking hands, she broke the seal. Each sentence, each word, stole strength from her legs, until she swayed.

Ben reached for her, his grip on her arm a steadying beam. "What is it?"

Betty retreated, taking the light with her. Light? La, as if any shone into this manor of despair.

"Clara?" Ben's voice sounded far away, somewhere overhead and fuzzy. "What's happened?"

She cleared her throat. How to make her voice work at a time such as this? "Aunt Mitchell is not doing well." The words came out jagged around the edges, but at least they came out. "The doctor says if I wish a good-bye, now is the time."

She stared, unseeing, into Ben's eyes.

He held her shoulders, firming her up on each side. "Then you must go."

Go? Were Aunt to die, then there was nothing for her anymore. Nowhere to go. No means to support herself. But if she stayed another day and a half at Bleakly, then she stood a good chance of being self-sufficient long enough to find another position.

Could Aunt hold on for that long?

Ben bent, peering closer. "What are you thinking?"

"If I leave now, I shall ruin my chances of five hundred pounds. I know that sounds callous and cold, but—" A sob welled in her throat. It sounded that way because it was. "Oh, Ben, what shall I do?"

"A last good-bye isn't worth any amount of money. It is priceless." Cupping her cheeks with his hands, he lifted her face. "I never got to say good-bye to you or my life before being cast away into Millbank."

The emotion in his gaze nearly choked her. "You're right, of course. Yes, I shall go. But I—"

She what? How to put into words the fear, the terror, of leaving him again? What kind of cruel joke was it to bring them together, then rip them apart for a second time? The dam burst, and hot tears scalded her cheeks.

Ben brushed them away with his thumbs. "What's this?"

"I–I shall miss you." Loss tasted as salty as the tears on her lips.

"As long as I draw breath, Clara, I vow I will go to you immediately after quitting this place. I swear it. Nothing, *nothing* will keep me from you." A muscle jumped on his jaw. Slowly he sank to one knee, pulling her hand to his lips. He kissed her so softly, she trembled. The hazel of his eyes burned up into hers. "Will you trust in me again? Will you allow me to show you how much I love you?"

Old memories of the pitiful stares, the whispered remarks as she stood alone on display in front of an altar, cut a fresh mark on her soul. How awful, how excruciating, to be burned twice over with the same fire. But was this time not completely different? *Oh God, please let it be so.*

She reached into her pocket and wrapped her fingers around the second-chance coin. Hesitating for only a breath, she held it out. "Perhaps this coin was never meant for me, but for you."

His fingers entwined with hers, and his throat bobbed as he took it.

"I will trust you, Benjamin Lane. But please. . ." Each word cost in ways that she'd pay for eternity if he failed her in this. "Do not break my heart again."

CHAPTER TWENTY-EIGHT

Feeble afternoon sunlight faded into early evening shadows, darkening the library. At a table near the door, Ben retrieved a candle lantern and lit it, his breath puffing a little cloud in the frigid chamber. No stranger to the cold, he tugged the lapels of his dress coat closer and strode from the room. Once Clara had departed, he'd spent the bulk of the day re-exploring the empty manor from cellar to rafters, hoping to find the reclusive master. All he'd discovered was Betty debating with two kitchen staff about the freshness of the fish for dinner, a stable hand who'd come in for a mug of ale, and countless locked doors that hid secrets. Blast! But he was sick of secrets.

Quickening his pace, he stalked from corridor to corridor, finally stopping in the empty front foyer. He widened his stance and faced the lion head.

"Why not end the charade now? I am the last one remaining. Show yourself and be done with it."

Lifeless eyes stared down at him. Not that he expected an answer—nor the sudden rap of the knocker on the front door.

Wheeling about, he cast aside convention and opened the door himself.

A ruddy-cheeked fellow with frosted eyebrows and a red-tipped nose stood at attention. "Is there a Mr. Lane in residence?"

"I am he."

"Excellent. This delivery is for you, sir." He held out a canvas messenger bag.

Ben rolled his eyes. This was too convenient. Too coincidental. He glanced over his shoulder, back up at the lion head, feeling more than ever like a pawn.

Yet what else was there to do at this point but finish the game?

Stifling a growl, he took the bag with a forced "Thank you," then rummaged around in his pocket for something to give the man. Nothing but Clara's second-chance coin met his touch. Ahh, but poverty was a cruel master, not only for him, but for the poor delivery man who'd have to trek back to God-knew-where with nothing but chapped skin to show for it.

Ben met the man's gaze. "I am sorry, but I'm afraid I have no tip."

"No need." The fellow swiped the moisture from the end of his nose with the edge of his sleeve. "I've been paid handsomely. Good night." He turned and jogged down the stairs, mounted a fine-looking bay, and trotted off into the twilight.

Closing the door on the cold, Ben tucked the bag under one arm and strode into the drawing room—the one chamber with a fire. He poured a glass of wine, then settled in the chair nearest the hearth as the mantel clock struck five. Untying the leather thong secured around two buttons, he opened the flap. Inside was a large packet, thick and weighty, and three smaller envelopes at the bottom. No, hold on. He fished his finger into one corner and pulled out a scrap of paper. Hasty penmanship scrawled across it, reading: *You don't have to be right. You just have to be.*

His brows pinched. What was that supposed to mean?

Setting it aside, he withdrew the envelopes and went first for the one that was unsealed. Dumping the contents onto his lap, he rifled through what appeared to be receipts. Many wrinkled. Some torn. All with large sums and different dates spanning the past nine months. A new top hat. A case of *Chateau Margaux*. Fees spent for villas and servants and travel arrangements to and from a spate of European countries. Ben shoved the papers back into the envelope. What had this to do with anything?

He paused to swallow a sip of his drink, then drew out the biggest packet and set the bag down on the floor. Perhaps by reading the rest he'd understand the cryptic scrap. Laying the folder on his lap, he flipped it open. Pages of parchment, lots of them, neatly penned. He picked up the first page, then gaped at the title written in black ink at the top: *Blythe vs Lane.*

A shock jolted through him as he read further. These were court documents. The papers he'd begged to see before, during, and after his trial. The key to discovering who'd brought embezzlement charges against him in the first place.

He rifled through the pile, scanning like a madman, revisiting the indictment, the verdict, discovering the names of the members of the jury, and finally the page naming the plaintiff. His hands shook. His whole body did. At last he'd know whom to seek out, whom to pay back all the horrors he'd had to live through the past nine months: *George Chapman.*

The paper slipped from his fingers. The name made no sense. Clara's brother, his friend and colleague, was his accuser?

He shoved the documents back into the bag and pulled out the other two envelopes. One felt heavier, so he opened that one first. A letter, folded into thirds, was addressed to High Court Justice Richard Combee.

Though his throat was parched, he ignored his glass of wine and shook out the missive, then skimmed the page. The first half was blotted in parts, the ink washed out where some sort of liquid had spilled onto the paper. It mostly looked like salutations anyway. But the words in the middle were clear enough:

> *. . .appreciate your handling with utmost confidentiality*
> *the matter of Benjamin Lane. As per our previous*
> *conversation, the sum of one thousand pounds shall*
> *be yours in exchange for his transportation.*
> *As always, your servant,*
> *George Chapman*

The paper crumpled in his hand as if his fingers squeezed about George's neck. It couldn't be helped. Such rage, when birthed, could not be shoved back inside any more than a babe could revisit a mother's womb. Of course he should have known—he just didn't want to. But it made perfect sense.

From the time they'd been lads, he and George had competed for everything, from trying to acquire the headmaster's praise before the other to rowing contests on the River Cam. Landing a partnership at the same shipping company, it was only natural they vied for the ultimate prize—the great Blythe warehouse industry. Had George somehow discovered he would not be the winner? The sweet after-taste of wine soured at the back of his throat. Were that conjecture true, that meant *he* would have been the one to take over the pros-perous business. Would George truly have been so heinous as to steal the money, cast the blame on him, and leave his own sister practically destitute?

Drawing in a deep breath to clear his head, he tucked the letter into the envelope and tossed back the rest of his drink. *Steady, steady.*

He opened the last envelope and pulled out a single half sheet. A block cut of a steamship adorned the left corner. At the right, writ-ten in red ink, the word *copy.* Across the top, the title of *Liverpool, London & Glasgow Packet Company* spread out in swirled letters. The line below that listed the destination—New York—and the departure date: January 5. Tomorrow, then. At ten in the morning. Berth No. 12. Balance due $0. Wapping Wharves. And the bearer's name—*George Chapman.*

Ben shot to his feet, the paper fluttering to the floor along with the messenger bag and the rest of the documents. Running both hands through his hair, he circled the room, heart racing. This was it. All he'd dreamed about for the past nine hellish months while rotting away in Millbank. Revenge in full. If he left now, he'd easily make it in time to London, to the docks, to the ship. He could drag George to a real court instead of the court of bogus justice Ben had endured—provided he could restrain himself from choking the life out of the scoundrel beforehand.

He stopped in front of the hearth and grabbed the mantel with both hands. If he stepped off Bleakly Manor property, he'd be shot for escape. Yet how else could he stop George? Once the rogue landed in America, there'd be no finding him. There'd be no justice. There'd be nothing but a grand life for George while he and Clara worked to scratch out a living.

Clara.

He hung his head and stared at the coals. He'd nearly forgotten his vow to her. Shoving his hand into his pocket, he pulled out the second-chance coin, then spun and glowered at the papers strewn on the floor.

If he walked out the door of Bleakly Manor, he'd face death—once again breaking his oath to Clara. The coin burned in his palm, and the need for righteousness in his gut.

There was freedom if he stayed. Revenge if he didn't.

Which one should he chance?

Twelfth Night Holiday

JANUARY 5, 1851

CHAPTER TWENTY-NINE

Morning light cast oblong rectangles on the rug in Aunt's chamber. Clara watched them shorten, her head bobbing now and then, jerking her back to wakefulness. The wicked tick-tock of the clock tempted her to close her eyes. Just for a moment. To forget the pinch of her corset and ache of her bones. Ahh, but she was weary from travel, from worrying, life, and the eleven long days she'd spent at Bleakly Manor. Shifting on the chair she'd occupied since she'd arrived last night, she rested her cheek against the wingback and surrendered with a sigh.

"You sound as if you bear the world on your shoulders." A paper-thin voice rustled on the air.

Bolting upright, she dashed to Aunt Mitchell's bedside and dropped to her knees. Set in a face the colour of milk paint, watery eyes stared at her, open and alive. "Oh, Aunt, how are you?"

Aunt's lips curved into a frail smile. "A sight better than you, by the looks of it."

Pulling her loosened hair back over her shoulder, Clara leaned closer and studied the rise and fall of Aunt's chest. The counterpane barely moved. She bit back a cry. "I've been so worried."

"La, child." A raspy gurgle in Aunt's throat accompanied her words. "Worrying doesn't stop the bad from happening. It keeps you from enjoying the good."

"What would I do without your wisdom?" The world turned watery, and Clara blinked to keep her tears locked up. "What *will* I do without you?"

The old lady's fingers fluttered toward her, inching across the top of the coverlet. Clara reached for her hand, hopefully saving Aunt whatever strength she might have left.

Aunt's squeeze was light as a butterfly's wing. "Now, now, chin up. I'm not gone yet."

"No, you are not." She swallowed against the tightness in her throat. "And for that I am thankful."

"But I am ready to go, child. I have lived a full life. My only regret is I have nothing to leave you. Wicked entailments." Releasing her hand, Aunt's fingers trembled upward, landing on Clara's cheek. "How I'd wished you to be mistress of this house."

Clara leaned into her touch. "I am sure Mr. Barrett will make a fine master."

"Master, yes. Fine? Hardly." Aunt's hand dropped to the bed, and her pale eyes flashed a spark—albeit tiny—of spunk. "Be thankful you never crossed paths with that side of my husband's family."

Great coughs rumbled in Aunt's chest, draining her of an already thin colour.

Clara darted to a side table and retrieved a glass of watered wine. Most dribbled down Aunt's chin, staining her white nightgown like drops of blood, but enough moistened her mouth that the hacking fit abated.

"Rest now. I shall be right here with you." Clara stood.

But Aunt's fingers beckoned her back. "Soon this body will do nothing but rest. Please, humour me. I should like to hear of your adventures at Bleakly Manor."

Frowning, she studied the woman. Bird bones wrapped in white linen couldn't have looked more fragile, yet a thread of strength remained in Aunt's voice.

"Very well." Taking care not to jostle the mattress overmuch, she sat on the edge of the bed and took Aunt's hands between both of hers. Once again the ticking clock taunted her, counting down the final minutes of Aunt's life. How to explain the strange characters she'd spent the past eleven days with?

Aunt's gaze sought hers. "Just tell me what's on your heart, child."

"Ben was there." The words blurted out before she could stop them, and she sucked in a gasp.

"Was he now?" Despite the glassy shadow of death, Aunt's eyes twinkled.

Twinkled?

Clara frowned at the odd response, suspicion growing stronger with each beat of her heart. "Why, you *knew* he'd be there. That's why you encouraged me to go, is it not?"

"My body fails, but my mind does not." Aunt pulled her hand away and tapped her head. "There's still a little intrigue left up here."

The movement loosed the demon in Aunt's chest, unleashing a spate of coughing. This was too much, despite what Aunt Mitchell desired.

Clara rose. "Rest now, Aunt. I vow I shall be here when you next awaken and we will talk more."

"No!" The old lady's head flailed on the pillow, her voice as mewling as a newborn kitten's. "There's something you need to know. Bleakly Manor was no coincidence and in fact was my last hope for your future."

Stunned, Clara blinked, her own voice quivering. "What are you saying?"

"It started last fall, September. Charles, a dear old friend of mine, called on me. He told me he was struggling to create his next hero and heroine." Pausing, Aunt licked her lips, white foam collecting at the edges.

Clearly she would not be put off, so Clara propped up Aunt's head and helped her drink, then sat at her side.

"Mmm. So good. Now, where was I?" For a moment, Aunt closed her eyes, and Clara wondered if she'd doze off finally.

But her lids popped open. "Charles is a writer. He had a story in mind, and the plot pleased him, but his characters were. . . How did he put it? *All flattened and blowsy, like a handful of crushed chaff given to the wind.* Such a wordy fellow." A small chuckle gurgled in Aunt's throat.

Prepared for another coughing fit, Clara tensed, hating the awful smell of the mustard poultice on her aunt's chest, hating even more the thought that the next fit might be her last.

Yet the old lady rallied, drawing in a big breath. "So Charles concocted an experiment to help him create vibrant, believable characters by observation. He had several other people in mind, but none qualified as true leads. There are no two truer hearts I know than yours and Mr. Lane's, and so I suggested the two of you."

"But how could you? Did you know where Ben was all this time?

That he was a convicted felon?"

"You and I both know he could never be capable of such a crime."

Clara shook her head, trying to make sense of the strange conversation. "Why did you not tell me of this sooner?"

"There were many logistics and legalities to arrange. And the timing had to be right—a friend of Charles owns Bleakly Manor and was about to sail for the continent on business. He offered Charles the use of his house. Some of his staff went with him. Others visited their own families during his absence. So Charles had to hire temporary replacements on limited funds. That left little in the budget for food, coal, or other necessities. He wasn't even certain until the last minute that his experiment would come together. I didn't want to get your hopes up only to see them dashed." Aunt's eyes leaked, dampening her cheek. "You've suffered enough."

Clara's jaw dropped. Understanding dawned as bright and clear as the late-morning sun leaching the last colour from Aunt's skin as it shone on her thin form. "I see. You hoped I'd receive the five hundred pounds as a means of support."

"No, child. I hoped that by reuniting with your Ben you'd receive love. Though you are brilliant at hiding your heart, I've long known you underestimate your own value. But that view of yourself is a lie. Each of God's creatures is inherently precious. And so you are." Aunt's head lifted, a flicker of passion in her gaze. "You have made this last year of my life a delight, easing my loneliness more than you'll ever know. And as my friend Charles says, 'No one is useless in this world who lightens the burden of it to anyone else.'"

Deep down, in a place within her heart locked with chains, something clicked. A door opened. An awful monster rushed out at her, one that had resided in her soul since the day her father had come home drunk and blamed her for her mother's death in childbirth, saying he'd trade her in an instant if he could only have her mother back from the grave.

Clara covered her face and wept away the memory, the hurt, the lies. Wept it all away. And suddenly, the whys of life didn't matter anymore, for the love of her aunt, of Ben, of her Creator, flooded in and chased that fiend away.

"Child?"

Sucking in a shaky breath, she bent and embraced her aunt, then pulled back. "Thank you. I am grateful for your words and your friend's words."

Dabbing away a last tear, she wondered if Aunt's friend had been surprised by all the things that went awry in the manor and the near-death mishaps. A question that would have to remain unasked, for if Aunt knew what had truly gone on, it would burden her unduly. Instead, Clara curved her mouth into a small smile. "I should like to meet this wise Charles of yours someday."

"Indeed." Aunt's head sunk deep into her pillow, and she closed her eyes. "Mr. Dickens is a wise man."

CHAPTER THIRTY

Ben paced circles in the drawing room, the spare light of a single candle his only source of illumination—save for the leftover glow of coals in the hearth and the thin line of grey on the outside horizon. Midnight had come and gone. His chance to stop George Chapman was gone as well.

Stopping in front of the window, he shoved his hand into his pocket and yanked out the second-chance coin, flipping it over and over in his hand. Regret choked him, leaving behind an acrid taste. He should've taken the risk yesterday. He should've raced down to that dock and never looked back. Three times he'd braved the cold and walked the vast length of the drive to the edge of Bleakly Manor property, debating the chance of a bullet for the sake of justice.

And three times he'd turned back.

What kind of coward did that?

Opening his hand, he stared fiercely at Clara's gift. How long would it take to wear it smooth like the stone he'd once kept at Millbank? Would he be sent back there, after all? Should he not take this last opportunity to run free? To escape?

He rolled the coin from knuckle to knuckle, the friction of the metal against his skin reminding him he was human, not some beast to be hunted. Not in Clara's eyes, at any rate. Not anymore. Wasn't her trust and love worth more than revenge? That's what he'd told himself yesterday. And yes, even now he knew it in his heart—but the blasted nagging doubts in his head would not be stilled.

Lifting his face to the sky, he studied the brilliant rays of sun painting streaks of pink against the grey, then closed his eyes.

"Hear me, God." His voice was as rugged as his emotions. "Though it kills me in every possible way, I surrender, here and now, any further thoughts of vengeance against George Chapman. Make things right. Make *me* right. I leave this matter in Your hands, where it's always been, despite my doubts and questions."

He shoved the coin back into his pocket and stalked from the room. Shadows crept out from corners, but weak light began to filter in. Taking the stairs two at a time, he dashed to his room, knowing exactly what must be done next. Regardless of a bullet in his back, he would go to Clara, for he'd promised he would. Or he would die in the trying.

He shrugged into his greatcoat, wrapped a scarf around his neck, then yanked down a hat atop his head, covering the tips of his ears. The walk to London would be long and cold.

If he made it past Bleakly lands.

Trotting down the stairs, he stopped in the great foyer and pivoted to the lion head. His hand snapped to his forehead in salute. "Thank you for your hospitality, such as it was."

Then he turned and strode to the door, ready to set foot on the next chapter of his life, be it a paragraph or a page.

But it was a sentence, and a short one at that.

"Mr. Lane, I presume?" A footman blocked his path—dressed in the same livery the servants had worn his first night here.

"Yes," he answered.

"Your carriage will arrive shortly, sir." The fellow's arm shot out, offering an envelope in his gloved hand. "Until then, this is for you."

Ben pulled the paper from the footman's fingers. The man immediately wheeled about, descended the stairs, and hopped up on the back step of a black-lacquered carriage, one clearly not meant for him.

No matter. His feet wouldn't move should he wish them to. The simple piece of parchment in his hand, folded and blotted with red wax at the center, weighted him in place. Perspiration dotted his brow as he ran his finger under the seal. Legal text filled the page, hard to read for the way the paper quivered in his hands, but three clear words stood out: *Writ of emancipation.*

The miracle in ink shook through him, and for a moment he leaned against the doorframe, closing his eyes. *Thank You, God.*

The jingle of harnesses pulled him from his thoughts. Blinking into the brilliant morning light, he saw a long-legged man entering the carriage. Just before the door shut, the fellow tipped his hat at Ben. Then the coach lurched into motion. Had that been his one and only glimpse of the master of Bleakly Manor? A nondescript, black-haired fellow in a houndstooth sack jacket and bowler hat?

Ben tore down the stairs, intent on thanking him, but the coachman laid into the horses, urging them into a run.

Ben stood in the drive, staring after the retreating coach, as alone as the night he'd arrived—but this time standing in the brilliance of sunshine and freedom.

Five Days Later

JANUARY 10, 1851

CHAPTER THIRTY-ONE

Aunt Mitchell's labored breathing made Clara's chest hurt. But it was the chiming of the clock that really cut into her heart, carving out a hollow. Another day born in darkness. January 10. Days past the festive season.

Slumping in her chair near the door of Aunt's chamber, she debated leaving to go have a good cry into her pillow. Since her childhood, she'd always waxed melancholy after the flurry of Christmas. The walls stripped of decoration. The house empty of guests and laughter. It was the lonely time of year. The barren. With naught to look forward to but short grey days and frigid black nights. Yet none of that bothered her this time, not with Aunt's life balancing on the thin line tied from breath to breath.

And the fact that Ben had not come for her. Again.

Despair spread over her like a rash, hot, prickly, and entirely familiar. She knew it as well as the skin on her bones. At least this time the only eyes to witness her shame and grief were those closed nearly in death. Why had she been so foolish as to open her heart to the same man who'd crushed it once before? Was it any better to wonder if he'd been recaptured? Or killed? Would that make the pain any less?

Pressing the heels of her hands to her eyes, she stopped up the tears begging for release and whispered, "Why, God? Why?"

"If you knew all the answers, there'd be no need for trust, little one."

She jerked upright in the chair and swiveled her head toward Aunt—just as harsh words gathered out in the hall, growing louder the longer she listened. Dorothea Cruff, Aunt's housekeeper, howled like a baying beagle keen on the hunt. Clara bit her lip and shot up a quick plea of repentance. Truly it was wicked of her to compare the woman to a dog, but even Aunt referred to Mrs. Cruff's chambers as *the howlery.* What poor servant was the housekeeper gnawing on at such an hour? Clara turned up the wick in her oil lamp, intending on finding out, when the door opened.

Mrs. Cruff's mobcapped head peeked through the gap. "Begging your pardon, Miss Chapman. But there's a gentleman, leastwise he says he is, who will not—"

The door shoved wider and, sidestepping Mrs. Cruff, in strode a broad-shouldered shape, draped in a black riding cloak and dark trousers. Mud bespattered him from toe to neck, little flecks of it falling to the floor as he doffed his hat.

But before lamplight caught on the man's burnt cream–coloured hair, Clara jumped up and plowed into him. "You came!"

Faltering back a step, Ben chuckled and wrapped his arms around her. "So it appears."

Listening to his heart beat against her ear, she stayed there, nuzzling her cheek against his chest, breathing in deeply of his scent, all smoky and with a whiff of horseflesh. He'd come. He'd really come for her. All the anguish and doubt of the past several days melted as she nestled into the heat of him.

" 'Tain't right. 'Tain't proper." Behind them, Mrs. Cruff scolded as proficiently as Mr. Tallgrass might have.

Unwilling to forfeit such a hard-won embrace, Clara turned yet did not step out of Ben's hold.

Mrs. Cruff's face could kill an entire battalion of dragoons with one glance, so fiercely did she scowl.

Clara fired back her own evil eye. "Light the lamps and see to a fire in the sitting room, if you please, Mrs. Cruff."

"No, I don't very well please, and furthermore—"

Ben released her and held up a hand. "No need. Thank you, but this shan't take long. You are dismissed."

The woman's mouth opened, a magnificent howl about to issue, when Aunt Mitchell's voice floated across the room.

"Go to bed, Cruff. I would speak with Clara and her gentleman."

The housekeeper's lips snapped shut. Silence escorted her out of the room until she reached the corridor, where a low grumbling began—and no doubt would accompany her all the way to the howlery.

With a gentle yet firm hand on the small of Clara's back, Ben ushered her to Aunt's bedside. "Sorry for the hour, Mrs. Mitchell. I came as soon as I could. Between a lame horse, a broken axle, and a downed tree at Hounslow, the journey took longer than expected. I am happy you are still among us."

Aunt nodded, an almost imperceptible movement, so delicate her constitution. "Your expected arrival is what's been keeping me alive."

Clara exchanged a glance with Ben. Did he know what she was talking about?

The arch of his brow said not. He pulled her down to kneel alongside him at Aunt's bedside.

Ben reached for the old lady's hand and cradled it in his, the contrast between vitality and weakness stark in the shadowy light. "I am sorry to bear unwelcome news, but I've discovered the truth behind what really happened with the Chapman fortune and Blythe shipping. Your nephew George stole all the funds, leaving me with the blame and you, Mrs. Mitchell, to care for Clara—for which I owe you my gratitude."

"No!" Clara sat back on her heels, the world tipping beneath her. "George would never...I mean...but he's gone to America. He's working even now to secure a place for me."

"No, my love." Amber eyes sought hers, and the compassion shining there nearly undid her. "In truth, your brother's been cutting a swath of decadent living across Europe. Only days ago did he sail for America."

"He did not." Aunt's frail voice pulled both their gazes back to her.

Ben leaned closer to the old woman, the lines on his face softening. "I am sorry to contradict you, madam, but—"

Aunt's fingers quivered upward, landing on his cheek. "If you are here, that means George did not sail for America but has been apprehended and will stand trial. You will be fully acquitted."

The words blew around Clara like a fine snow caught in an eddy of wind. In truth, she felt just as swirly. Was everything she'd believed for nearly the past year nothing but lies?

She huddled closer to Ben, hoping to draw strength from the sheer closeness of his broad shoulders. "Aunt, what are you saying?"

Air rattled in the old lady's lungs as she drew in a breath. "I long had my suspicions about your brother, but no evidence until recently."

Aunt's fingers dropped to the sheets. "George is not your full brother, my dear. He's but a half. His mother refused to marry your father, wild in all her ways. Despicable woman. I feared George would turn out like her, but one cannot accuse based on bad character alone. I needed proof."

Aunt's eyes closed, and her chest fluttered.

So did Clara's pulse. All she'd known, all she'd assumed, vanished, replaced with keen comprehension. She'd understood her father's coldness toward her because her mother had died in the birthing, but her father's detachment toward George had always been a puzzlement. Until now. No wonder she'd always felt the odd goose with her raven hair and olive skin, standing next to her brother, so fair in colour and handsome looks.

A chill crept across her shoulders, and she shivered.

Ben pulled her closer to his side and patted Aunt's hand. "We shall leave you to rest."

"Not yet." Aunt's eyelids flickered open. "You must know. My friend, Charles, rubs shoulders with powerful men. One, a barrister with a sharp sense of justice." She paused, her tongue working to moisten her lips.

Clara pulled away and retrieved a cloth she kept dipped in water, then patted it against her aunt's mouth.

A faint smile lifted one side of the old lady's lips. "That barrister labored to trade Ben's transportation for house arrest at Bleakly, then worked the holiday season to gather all the evidence by Twelfth Night."

Her words stalled, and Ben leaned closer, bending his ear toward her mouth. "Are you saying I have been acquitted this whole time?"

"No. Had you tried to escape or gone after George, you would have been shot for evasion." Aunt's head shook like the last leaf in autumn. "Yet I vouched for your character, my son."

Ben reared back to his heels, nostrils flaring as he sucked in a breath. "But why?"

A flare of brightness lit Aunt Mitchell's eyes, for a moment driving colour into her whitewashed cheeks. "I never had children of my own, but I couldn't have loved them any more dearly than Clara and you. Promise me. . .promise. . ."

Rattles traveled from Aunt's chest to her throat, and both Clara and Ben leaned in close.

With a last rally, Aunt reached for Ben's hand and moved it to Clara's. "Take care of my Clara."

Ben's strong fingers encased both of theirs. "I vow it." He squeezed, gently. "This night and for always."

Aunt closed her eyes, her hand going limp in theirs. It wouldn't be long before she left the land of the living.

Grief welled in Clara's throat, and she pulled her hand free to press a knuckle against her mouth, trapping the noise.

Ben tucked the old lady's fingers beneath the bedsheet, then pulled Clara up along with him. "Come," he whispered, then led her, hand in hand, to the corridor and closed the door behind them.

Emotions assailed her, one after the other. Sorrow. Confusion. But above all a sense of duty to the man walking beside her. She stopped and turned to Ben. "You have been restored, and for that I am truly grateful, but please, despite what was said, do not feel obligated to keep such a promise to Aunt."

She tried to pull away from his grasp, but he merely captured her other hand and rubbed his thumbs along the inside curve of her palms. "Surely you know you are more than an obligation to me."

"But I am penniless! George saw to that by spending the money." Her voice caught, and she hung her head. "No one will welcome me back into their circles. I have fallen from grace."

"Yet it is grace alone that saves the worst of us." He released his hold and worked to shove up one of his sleeves. Blackened numbers, charred into his skin, stared up at her.

A single tear broke loose, landing on the hideous brand. She brushed it away, her finger traveling over the seared flesh. How could he love so much after having suffered because of her brother? Her throat nearly closed at the thought of such depth, such rock-solid devotion—to her.

He reached into his pocket and pulled out the coin, then pressed it into her hand. "And it was your grace that gave me a second chance."

Pulling her to him, he slid his strong hands upward to cup the back of her head. For a second, he hesitated, caressing her with a gaze that made her his own. Then his mouth came down, meeting hers, claiming her in deed. By the time he pulled away, breathing was out of the question.

"I am a free man now, Clara, and in time, the Court of Chancery will fully restore my family estate. All this gain, though, is empty without you. And so I must know"—his voice lowered, crackling with love and desire—"will you have a former convict as a husband?"

Tears would not be stopped, the taste of them salty on her lips. Oh, how she'd missed this man, this love, this part of her that had been torn and was now mended stronger than before. She smiled up at him, realizing that, indeed, she may never stop smiling for the rest of her years. "I would have none other than you, my love."

Two Weeks Later

JANUARY 24, 1851

CHAPTER THIRTY-TWO

A cold mist settled over London, dampening everyone's clothing to the same shade of dreary. It was the kind of late January day that crawled under the best of woolen capes and took up residence in the bones. In Cheapside, old men huddled at their hearths. On Aldred Street, mothers sheltered younglings beneath great black umbrellas.

But in Holywell, Clara stepped lively down the narrow lanes, ignoring the chill.

Stopping in front of Effie Gedge's door, she raised her hand and rapped, then smiled at the smudge left behind on her glove. It would be the last time this ragtag collection of boards marred her bleached kidskin.

The door swung open, and Effie's sweet face appeared—cheekbones prominent, skin sallow, yet her ever-present smile fixed in place. "Miss Chapman! What a grand surprise." The girl's brows drew together, and she dared a step closer despite the rain that would catch on her hair. "But what are you doing here? Is all well?"

"No. . .and yes. So much has happened in the past month, I hardly know where to begin." She'd never spoke truer words. Biting the inside of her cheek, she searched for some nicely packaged phrases, as she had during the entire ride over here, but still none came to mind. How to speak of passions and sorrows so great?

"My aunt Mitchell has died," she blurted.

"Oh! I am so sorry." Effie reached out and grabbed her arm, as if to impart strength—quite the absurdity from a woman worn to threads by circumstance. "She were a rare one, weren't she?"

"That she was." Clara fought back a fresh wave of tears, though should any slip, they could easily be blamed upon the mist.

"It's not much, miss, but I'm sure I can get you into the factory. It won't be easy, mind you. Hatbox work is hard on the hands, but it's a fair sight easier than being a silk piecer or a salt boiler, and far better than starving." Effie shoved the door wider, lips curving into a welcome. "You can share my room, though we'll have to snug up in the bed, for I've only space enough for that and a chair."

Though the January day did its worst to inflict a shiver, Clara pressed a hand to her chest, warmed through the heart at Effie's kindness. "Oh, Effie, you are the rare one. I did come here to ask you something, but not that." Loosening the drawstring on her reticule, she pulled out the second-chance coin and pressed it into Effie's reddened hands.

Effie looked from the gold piece to Clara. "What's this for?"

"It's a second-chance coin."

"A what?"

Clara smiled. How many times had she wondered the very same thing? "I am here to ask you for a second chance. Would you consider coming back as my maid? There is much to be done, and I could use your help."

"I don't understand." A tremor shook Effie's head, though hard to tell if the movement was from the cold or confusion. "I thought once your aunt was deceased, the house and all her means passed on to her stepson. Don't tell me you and him. . . ?"

"No, nothing of the sort. That is not the household I am asking you to serve."

"Then whose?"

Her grin widened, for whenever she thought of Ben, a smile must be allowed. "Mr. Benjamin Lane's household, my soon-to-be husband. We have a wedding to prepare for. Are you up to it? It won't be easy, but it's a fair sight easier than hatbox making—and you won't have to share your bed." She winked. "What do you say?"

Effie beamed. "I say let our new lives begin!"

Historical Notes

Victorian Christmas Traditions

The Twelve Day Celebration
Since medieval times, the Twelve Day celebration has been a recognized holiday. It traditionally begins on Christmas Day, December 25, and ends at midnight, January 5, immediately before Epiphany.

Boxing Day
This holiday is celebrated the day after Christmas Day. Tradesmen and servants receive gifts from their masters, employers, or customers. These gifts are boxed up, hence the name Boxing Day.

The Yule Log
A Yule log was dragged in on Christmas Day and kept burning for twelve days (until Epiphany). The leftover charcoal was kept until the following Christmas to kindle the next year's log. It was considered bad luck if the log went out during the Twelve Days.

Childermas
December 28 is known as Holy Innocents' Day or Childermas. It's a day commemorating when King Herod ordered the murder of children under two years of age in an attempt to kill the baby Jesus. The "Coventry Carol" recounts the massacre from the eyes of a mourning mother whose child was killed. The song was commonly sung by itinerant carolers.

New Year's Coin
No matter the age, it was a must that every person in Victorian England should have money in his or her pocket on New Year's Day, even something as small as a half farthing (worth an eighth of a penny). To be without a coin meant risking poverty in the coming year.

Traveling Entertainers
During the Christmas season, entertainers traveled from manor to

manor. The most common form of their performances was panto-mime, which is still a popular form of entertainment today during the holidays.

Wassail
Originally, wassail was a greeting or a toast. Revelers would hold up a mug of spiced cider and shout, "Waes hael!" which means *be hale* or *be well*. The drink was often offered to visitors in a large wooden bowl. Eventually, the greeting fell by the wayside and wassail came to mean the drink instead of the toast. Many great traditional wassail recipes can be found on the Internet. Here is one of my favorites: http://www .curiouscuisiniere.com/wassail-recipe/.

DEDICATION

To the One and Only who gives mankind
a second chance—Jesus Christ.
And to Deborha Mitchell, the namesake of Clara's aunt.

ACKNOWLEDGMENTS

Writing is a solitary profession that cannot be done alone.
Thank you to Annie Tipton and the awesome staff at Shiloh Run
who continually make my writing dreams come true. A shout-out
to my long-suffering critique partners: Lisa Ludwig, Ane Mulligan,
MaryLu Tyndall, Julie Klassen, Shannon McNear, and Chawna
Schroeder. . .ALL talented authors in their own right. And as always,
my gratitude to Mark, who endures many a frozen pizza
and Chinese take-out when it's crunch time.

*Plus a special thank-you to you, readers,
who make this writing gig all worthwhile!*

ABOUT THE AUTHOR

Michelle Griep has been writing since she first discovered blank wall space and Crayolas. She seeks to glorify God in all that she writes—except for that graffiti phase she went through as a teenager. She resides in the frozen tundra of Minnesota, where she teaches history and writing classes for a local high school co-op. An Anglophile at heart, she runs off to England every chance she gets under the guise of research. Really, though, she's eating excessive amounts of scones and rambling through some castle. Keep up with her adventures at her award-winning blog "Writer Off the Leash" or visit michellegriep .com. She loves to hear from readers, so go ahead and rattle her cage.

Coming fall 2018

The journey continues in. . .

A Tale of Two Hearts

Book 2 in the Once Upon a Dickens Christmas series

A Novel by Michelle Griep

ENJOY THIS EXTENDED PREVIEW!

CHAPTER ONE

London, 1853

W hether I shall turn out to be the hero of my own life, or whether
that station will be held by anybody else, these pages must show."

Mina Scott lowered the copy of *David Copperfield* to her lap and
lifted her face to the October sun. Closing her eyes, she savored the
warmth and the first line to a new adventure, as was her wont whenever old lady Whymsy lent her a book. Though she no longer stared at
the page, the shapes of the words lingered, blazed in stark contrast to
the sun's brilliance against her lids. What a curious thought, to be one's
own hero—for the only hero she wanted was William Barlow.

Ahh, William. Just thinking his name lit a fire in her belly.

"Mina!"

She shot to her feet, and the book plummeted to the ground. Her
stomach dropped along with it—for being caught idle, and for the dirt
smudges sure to mar the cover. With her toe, she quickly slid the novel
beneath her skirt hem, then turned to face her father.

Jasper Scott, master of the Golden Egg Inn and commander of her
life, fisted hands the size of kidney pies at his hips. "What are ye doin'
out in the yard, girl, when ye ought be serving?"

"It's hardly teatime, Father. I thought to take a break before customers arrived." From the peak of the inn's rooftop, a swallow not yet
flown to warmer climates chided her for a lame excuse. Not that she
blamed the bird, for it was a pitiful defense, indeed.

Her father's bushy brows pulled into a single line. "Don't tell me
you were reading again."

How did he know? How did he *always* know?

"I. . ." She tucked her chin, debating the greater evil—lying or
disobedience?

Slowly, she bent and retrieved the book, then held it out. "Maybe you ought to keep this until we close tonight."

"I thought as much when Mrs. Whymsy stopped by. Keep your head in the world, girl, not in the clouds." He snatched the novel from her hand. "Now off with ye. There's already patrons clamoring for a whistle wetting."

She scurried past him and darted through the back door, nearly crashing into Martha, the inn's cook.

"Peas and porridge!" Martha quickly stepped aside, the water in her pot sloshing over the rim and dampening the flagstones. "Watch yer step, missy!"

"Sorry, Martha." Giving the lady a wider berth, she dashed to a peg on the wall and took down her apron. She made short work of tying the waistband and tucking in an extra cloth for wiping tables, then scooted to the taproom door before her father could find reason to scold her further.

Once she entered the public area, she slowed her steps and drew in a deep breath. No one liked to be waited upon by a ruddy-cheeked snippet of a skirt. Scanning the room, she frowned. Only two tables were filled. Surely Father could have managed to wait upon these few—

Her gaze landed on her golden-haired hero, ramping up her heartbeat to a wild pace. His broad back toward her, in deep conversation with the fellow seated next to him, William Barlow changed the entire ill-lit taproom to a brilliant summer landscape simply by merit of his presence—and his laugh.

Mina grabbed a pitcher and quickly filled it with ale, the pull of William too strong to deny. Bypassing the other customers, she headed straight for his table.

"He's invited me to a tea, of all things. Me!" His voice, smooth as fresh-flowing honey and just as pleasant, grew louder the closer she drew to his table. "Can you imagine that, Fitz? A tea. How awful."

A smile curved her mouth, imagining taking tea with William. Just the two of them. She'd pour a cup for him. He'd lift a choice little cake to her lips while speaking of his deepest affections. She sighed, warm and contented. "I should think a tea would be very pleasant," she murmured.

Both men turned toward her. Mr. Fitzroy, William's friend, spoke first. "Well, if it isn't the lovely Miss Scott, come to save me from this boorish fellow." He nudged William with his elbow.

William arched a brow at her, a rogue grin deepening the dimples at the sides of his mouth. "I was wondering when you'd grace us with your appearance, sweet Mina."

Sweet Mina. Heat flooded her cheeks. She'd be remembering that endearment in her dreams tonight.

But for now, she scowled. "Mr. Barlow, if my father hears of your familiarity, I fear—"

"Never fear, my sweet." He winked—and her knees weakened. "I'm a champion with ruffled fathers."

Ignoring his wordplay, she held up the pitcher. "Refills?"

William slapped his hand to his heart. "You know me too well."

Not as well as I'd like to. La! Where had that come from? Maybe Father was right, and she had been reading too many books.

"I'm as intrigued as Miss Scott." Mr. Fitzroy held his cup out to her, for she'd filled William's mug first. "Why would you not want to attend your uncle's tea? As I recall, he's a jolly-enough fellow."

William slugged back a long draw of his ale, then lowered his cup to the table. "Nothing against Uncle Barlow, mind you. It's just that I'm to bring my wife along."

Wife!

Mina's pitcher clattered to the floor. She stared at it, horrified. Ale seeped into the cracks of the floorboards, the very image of her draining hopes and dreams. William had a wife?

He shot to his feet. "Mina! You look as if you've seen the Cock Lane ghost. Are you ill?"

"I'm f–fine. The pitcher—it slipped, that's all." She crouched, yanking the rag from her waistband and mopping up the mess with more force than necessary. The rogue! The scoundrel! All this time he'd been trifling with her when he already had a hearth and home tended by a wife? Did he have children, as well? She scrubbed harder. Her knuckles grazed the rough wood and scraped her skin. Good. She relished the pain and, for a wicked moment, thought about swishing the spilled ale over William's shoes.

"Wife?" Surprise deepened Mr. Fitzroy's voice also. So. . .William's best friend had not known, either? That was a small satisfaction, at least.

"This is news," Mr. Fitzroy continued. "When did that happen?"

Holding her breath, she strained to hear, though why she cared indicted her for being naught but a dunderheaded hero seeker. *Silly girl. Silly, stupid girl.*

William sank back to his seat. "Well, I don't actually have one yet. And that's the problem."

"Thank God." The words flew out before she could stop them. She bit her lip. If Father heard her brazen speech, he'd take away more than her book.

William's face appeared below the table. "Are you quite all right?"

"Yes. Just finishing up." She forced a smile and reached for the runaway pitcher, then stood. This afternoon was turning into a novel in its own right. For the first time since she'd met William, she couldn't decide if he were truly a hero or a villain.

William straightened, as well, his gaze trained on her. The sun slanted through the front window, angling over his strong jaw and narrow nose. But it was his eyes that drew her. So brilliant, so true blue, a sob welled in her throat. She swallowed. She truly was a silly girl.

"Say, Mina," he drawled, "you wouldn't be willing to be my bride, would you?"

"I. . .I. . ." The words caught in her throat like a fish bone, and she coughed, then coughed some more. Heat blazed through her from head to toe. Surely, she hadn't heard right.

William's grin grew, his dimples deepening to a rakish angle. "Oh, don't panic. It would just be for the day."

Mr. Fitzroy leaned back, studying them both. "What's this all about, Will? For as long as I've known you, you've run from matrimony, not toward it."

"Oy, miss! Another round over here." Across the taproom, a stout fellow, buttons about to pop off his waistcoat, held a mug over his head.

William reached out and grasped her sleeve. "Please, Mina. This won't take but a moment."

A frown tugged her lips. Father wouldn't like her dawdling with William, but how could she refuse the man she'd cast as the champion in every story she'd read?

She glanced over her shoulder, nodding at the customer with a brilliant smile to stave him off, then turned back to William. "Make haste. I have work to attend to."

"Right. Here's the thing." He leaned forward, the excitement in his tone pulling both her and Mr. Fitzroy closer to him so that they huddled 'round the table.

"My uncle Barlow is ready to choose who will inherit his property. It's between me and my cousin Percy—"

"Egad!" Mr. Fitzroy rocked back on his chair. "That pompous hind end? I should think there'd be no competition whatsoever."

"I agree, but my uncle favors a married man. And since I am not..." Will tugged at his collar, loosing his cravat. "Well, I gave Uncle Barlow the impression I'd recently wed, or I'd not even be considered."

Mr. Fitzroy let out a long, low whistle.

Mina's eyes widened. "You lied to your uncle?"

William shook his head, the tips of his hair, long past needing a trim, brushing against his shoulders. "No, not outright. I merely led him on a merry word chase, and he arrived at a particular conclusion."

Mr. Fitzroy chuckled. "One day, my friend, your deceptions will catch up to you."

"Perhaps. But not today. Not if you, my sweet Mina"—William captured her free hand and squeezed—"will agree to be my wife for the tea. What do you say?"

Say? How could she even think when savoring the warmth of his fingers wrapped around hers? The blue of his gaze entreated her to yield to him. It would be lovely to live a fairy-tale life if only for an afternoon, take tea in a grand house—

"Miss!" the man across the room bellowed again.

And escape the drudgery of serving corpulent patrons who more often than not smelled of goats and sausages.

Pulling her hand away, she smiled at William. "I say yes."

She sucked in a breath. God bless her—for surely her father wouldn't.